DUTY TO DIE

JANICE THOMPSON

PROMISE
PRESS
An Imprint of Barbour Publishing

Published by Promise Press, an imprint of Barbour Publishing, Inc., P.O. Box 719, Uhrichsville, Ohio 44683, www.promisepress.com

 Member of the
Evangelical Christian
Publishers Association

Printed in the United States of America.

"Thompson makes vivid the outcome of the slippery slope from a 'right' to die to a 'duty' to die in a story that we should all hope will not become a reality."

(MRS.) TERRY SCHLOSSBERG
Executive Director
Presbyterians Pro-Life

"As we are seeing more and more commercials promoting 'choice' this novel opens our eyes to just where 'choice' may lead. . .a must read for anyone dealing with end of life issues.

"I feel that in due time our nation devoid of moral restraint and a church that will or won't pray diligently on these important issues will reveal whether *Duty to Die* remains a novel or becomes a prophetic piece of literature."

REV. GARY L. BARNES,
President, We Care Ministries, Inc.
Serving the Elderly, the Handicapped,
the Needy, and their Caregivers since 1991

DEDICATION

*This book is dedicated to
all of those who were taken before their time,
and to those like Ray and Lana Sanders, Jeanene Hanna,
and the others at CPC Central, Huston,
who have invested their time, energy, and resources into saving lives.
May God bless you in your work for Him.*

*Special thanks and all of my love to my husband, Michael,
and my beautiful daughters, Randi, Courtney, Megan, and
Courtney Elizabeth, who were willing to give me the time
and encouragement I needed to weave this little tale.
I love you all.*

Prologue

Is it possible that the so-called "right" to die will eventually become the "duty" to die? Consider the following historical timeline. . . .

935 B.C.: The Word of God declares that there is "a time to be born and a time to die. . . ." This "time" (according to Scripture) is clearly determined by the Lord. (Ecclesiastes 3:2 NIV)

585–580 B.C.: According to the prophet Jeremiah, the Lord knows us, even before our birth: "Before I formed you in the womb I knew you, before you were born I set you apart; I appointed you. . . ." (Jeremiah 1:5 NIV)

300 B.C.: The Hippocratic oath sets the standard for centuries to come. Among its precepts. . .the opposition to abortion, and the understanding that physicians will "do no harm."

13th Century: Thomas Aquinas speaks out concerning all forms of suicide, condemning it for the following reasons: "It violates one's natural desire to live; it harms other people; life is the gift of God and is thus only to be taken by God." (www.religioustolerance.org; from *The Catholic Encyclopedia*)

1823: In colonial America, courts and early state legislatures prohibit assisting in the act of suicide. "[I]f one counsels another to commit suicide, and the other by reason of the advice kills himself, the advisor is guilty of murder as principal." (Z. Swift, *A Digest of the Laws of the State of Connecticut,* 270)

1859: Charles Darwin's *The Origin of Species* is released, forever changing the scientific world's thinking concerning the origin and value of human life.

1920: *The Permission to Destroy Life Unworthy of Life* (authors Alfred Hoche, M.D., and Karl Binding) is published. It provides for the "allowable, useful act" of killing disabled adults and babies.

1920: Margaret Sanger (founder of Planned Parenthood) speaks in favor of contraceptives and against abortion: "The woman who has undergone an abortion is not altogether safe from harm. . . . Frequent abortions tend to cause barrenness and serious, painful pelvic ailments. These and other conditions arising from such operations are very likely to ruin a woman's general health." (Margaret Sanger, *Contraceptive or Abortion, Woman the New Race,* 1920)

1920–1930s: More from Margaret Sanger: "We do not want word to get out that we want to exterminate the Negro population." (*Margaret Sanger: Father of Modern Society* by Elasah Drogin)

1933: BERLIN, Oct. 7—The Ministry of Justice, in an attempt to explain the aims of the Nazi party, announces its intention to authorize physicians to end the sufferings of incurable patients. (Ohio Right to Life)

1934: "Feeble-minded persons, habitual congenital criminals, those afflicted with inheritable diseases, and others found biologically unfit should be sterilized or in cases of doubt be isolated as to prevent the perpetuation of their afflictions by breeding." (Margaret Sanger, *Code to Stop the Overproduction of Children,* 1934, p.71)

1939: The Nazi program "Aktion T4" sets out to eliminate "life unworthy of life." The program, at its onset, focuses on infants and very young children. Any child up to age three that shows symptoms of deformity must be registered with the Reich Health Ministry. Registry will, of course, prove to be a death sentence for many. (*The Origins of Nazi Genocide: From Euthanasia to the Final Solution.* Chapel Hill, N.C.: University of North Carolina Press, 1995)

1973: *Roe v. Wade* opens the door to legalized abortions in America. From that date forth, approximately 1.5 million children will "legally" lose their lives in America each year. (Statistics are based on research published by the Alan Guttmacher Institute, special research affiliate of Planned Parenthood Federation of America.)

1980: The Hemlock Society is formed, advocating the "right" to die and promoting physician-assisted suicide.

1989: The U.S. Civil Rights Commission examines the issue of euthanasia as it concerns infants and children with disabilities. It becomes increasingly more apparent that defective newborns are targeted for infanticide.

1990: "The slight, gray-haired man marched into the offices of the *Daily Tribune* of Royal Oak one spring day in 1990, introduced himself as a retired pathologist and said he wanted to place this ad: 'Jack Kevorkian, M.D. Bioethics and Obitiatry. Special death counseling. By appointment only.' Showing a photograph of a glass-and-tubing contraption he'd made from $30 worth of scrap parts, Kevorkian said it was a suicide machine and announced: 'I want to help people who want to end their lives.' " ("Kevorkian shows love-hate relationship with publicity," *Detroit Free Press,* Ariana E. Cha, March 7, 1997)

1990: The following article appears in a Detroit paper: "Applications are being accepted. Oppressed by a fatal disease, a severe handicap, a crippling deformity? Write Box 261, Royal Oak, Mich. 48068-0261. Show him proper compelling medical evidence that you should die, and Dr. Jack Kevorkian will help you kill yourself, free of charge." ("In Royal Oak: The Death Machine," *Detroit Free Press*, March 18, 1990, p. 24)

1990: Concerning those who are unable to choose death for themselves, Kevorkian states the following: "Infants, children, and others incapable of giving direct or informed consent are among the potential candidates for the humane killing known as euthanasia." He calls this "suicide by proxy." (Kevorkian, *Prescription, Medicide,* p. 200)

1991: Derek Humphry, founder of the Hemlock Society, writes his book *Let Me Die Before I Wake: Hemlock's Book of Self-deliverance for the Dying.*

1991: Speaking on the issue of euthanasia, C. Everett Koop, M.D., former Surgeon General of the United States says: "We must be wary of those who are too willing to end the lives of the elderly and the ill. If we ever decide that a poor quality of life justifies ending that life, we have taken a step down a slippery slope that places all of us in danger. . . . The call for euthanasia surfaces in our society periodically, as it is doing now under the guise of 'death with dignity' or assisted suicide." (*Koop: The Memoirs of America's Family Doctor* by C. Everett Koop: M.D., Random House, 1991)

1992: The Dutch Pediatric Association announces that it will issue formal guidelines for killing severely handicapped newborns.

1996: The death of a thirty-three-year-old HMO patient is revealed. He dies of suffocation on the floor of his bathroom as his wife frantically begs their HMO for permission to call for an ambulance. She is turned down. (The HMO Page; "Physicians Who Care"; http://www.hmopage.org/index.html)

1996: "Not Dead Yet" (a national disabilities rights group) is founded. Members recognize the fact that their disabilities put them at risk, and they stand opposed to the legalization of assisted suicide and euthanasia.

1996: Appearing on the April 12–14 cover of *USA Today* is the story of an unborn child with a gene for cystic fibrosis. The family's HMO agrees to cover the cost of an abortion but not the cost of care for the child should parents choose to let the child live.

1997: The state of Oregon enacts the Death with Dignity Act (DWDA), legalizing physician-assisted suicide (PAS).

1997: Oregon, having become the first state to legalize physician-assisted suicide, decides to offer this service to 270,000 low-income residents at no charge. ("Free Ticket to Eternity," *Washington Post,* Nat Hentoff, February 6 1999, p. A21)

1997: June 26—The Supreme Court rules that the so-called "right to die" has no constitutional basis and returns the matter to the jurisdiction of the states. Oregon implements "Death with Dignity," and the killing begins.

1999: Oregon's Death with Dignity Act Annual Report 1999 states that "during 1998, the first year of implementation, 23 Oregonians received prescriptions for lethal doses of medication; 15 of them died after ingesting these medications. . . . In 1999, 33 prescriptions were written for lethal doses of medication, and 27 patients participated in legal PAS (26 of the 33 1999 prescription recipients and one 1998 prescription recipient). (Oregon Health Division, Center for Health Statistics and Vital Records)

2000: June 28—The U.S. Supreme Court ruling strikes down (5 to 4) the Nebraska law banning partial-birth abortions. Infants in the very process of birth are now allowed to be murdered during delivery.

2000: September 28—The U.S. government (FDA) approves the use of the abortion pill RU-486, a major victory for abortion-rights advocates. The murder of an innocent child in the United States of America suddenly becomes even more controversial.

WHERE ARE WE NOW?

The world sits hunchbacked, waiting. . .anticipating what looks to be an ongoing slip down a dark, steep, well-oiled pathway toward destruction. We are, in many ways, just one law, one ruling away from the "duty" to die. But, just as in days of old, there are those nearby, perched, ready. . .to stand in the gap.

*Faithless is he that says farewell
when the road darkens.*

J. R. R. Tolkien

ONE

Drip, drip, drip. . .

Ashley Cooper gazed helplessly at the IV bag to her right. Her eyes were hypnotically fixed to it, as if in an unyielding trance.

Drip, drip, drip. . .

On and on it flowed, the methodical sound oddly soothing. Ashley's fingertips began to tap in sync on the rail of the hospital bed, eyes never losing their focus on the opaque bag. It was full of the clear, deadly mixture that was about to carry her over the edge—out of this life and into another.

Or was there another? Ashley wasn't really sure. Funny. Up to this moment, she hadn't given it much thought. It hadn't seemed terribly important. Was anything important anymore? Or was life just a mundane dragging from one day to the next? Was there a point to all of this?

A news reporter with a somewhat monotone voice spoke from the television, distracting her momentarily—but only momentarily. Ashley found it hard to focus on him, his voice disappearing into whispered nothingness. She turned her attention to the window, head moving in slow motion, eyes following.

A glimmer of sunlight peeked through the dusty venetian blinds, dancing its way across the room. It brought out the red in Ashley's long mane of hair, causing a curious glow to pass over her. The gentle radiance was warm, inviting. Ashley watched, transfixed, as the colors drifted from red to orange, then yellow, finally dissolving into a dismal haze. All of the vibrant hues seemed to be draining from the room now, replaced with varying shades of gray. The medicine was taking its toll.

Help me! Someone help me! Ashley tried to formulate the words, but couldn't seem to. In spite of the drug stupor, the young woman's mind continued to race. Where was she, again? Why was she here? There was death in this room. She could smell it, taste it, sense it all around her.

Is anyone listening?

There was so much she wanted to say! Was there still time? Could anyone hear? Nervously her eyes searched the room over. Was she alone? No one should have to pass through death's door alone! No, thank God, a nurse in starched white stood nearby, checking the monitor that was attached to the IV stand. But who was she—friend or foe? Was she here to help, or. . .

Help me, please!

Ashley's eyes briefly passed by the monitor. Was that her heartbeat? The somewhat rhythmic pattern repeated itself over and over again on the digital screen. The numbers were gradually dropping as the painkillers did their work to put her into a deep sleep.

So this is what dying is like. . . .

It was different than the frightened young woman had imagined, somehow. Ashley felt more alone than in all of her twenty-seven years. She wanted it to hurry. No, she wanted it to slow down.

Funny. She didn't know what she wanted anymore. Maybe she didn't even care. What was there to care about? Ever since the diagnosis, life had grown more and more meaningless.

The diagnosis.

This memory was crystal clear. Ashley began to tremble uncontrollably, remembering that eventful day—the day she had received the news that was to forever change her life—and her death.

"I'm so sorry, Miss Cooper. You have. . ."

Cancer. Incurable.

Prognosis: death.

The shock of it had sent her into an immediate panic. She, of all people, knew the implications. Her own father had died of cancer just eighteen months before. But now. . .

The law. . .

The law that had taken the right to die and turned it into a duty—"Duty to Die." No more would the decision be left in the hands of the individual, or even family members. The government would now decide who would live and who would die. This bill, recently passed in Congress, had instantly rendered incurable patients subject to mandatory euthanasia.

Incurable.

Another word for "financial burden to society." That's all Ashley had become in the eyes of the medical and political world. Her life was of no value now. She had nothing left to give—at least that's what they told her. Thirty short days were all she had been given to obtain a second opinion, make an informed decision about which plan she would opt for, sign the necessary forms for organ donation, and help family members with the arrangements for her own funeral.

A lonely tear trickled down Ashley's cheek as she tried to push their hurtful words from her memory.

A burden to society?

Hardly. A well-known corporate executive, Ashley Cooper was respected from Wall Street to Hollywood. Not a burden—an asset. But none of that mattered now. She was just a number, just a statistic. How had it come to this? Had she, like so many others, blinded herself to the reality of what was going on in the world around her?

Choices?

She had none. There was no time for choices, anyway. The inevitable was upon her. The medication was pulling, tugging. . . Ashley tried to relax, to let the power of the moment pull her in. She was drifting. . . .

In. Out. In. Out.

The silence in the room was overwhelming. Only the gentle ticking of the clock on the wall could distract her from the. . .

Drip, drip, drip. . .

Ashley's head slowly turned in the direction of the large wall clock. It, like everything else in the room, seemed to be more distant than before, harder to focus on for long. The power of the pull was overwhelming. Like a scene from an old movie, sepia tones in slow motion. . .Ashley sat as a spectator, unable to intervene on her own behalf.

10:21.

Drip, drip, drip. . .

The IV continued its steady current. If only she could stop it!

Tick, tick, tick. . .

The clock on the wall continued to beckon her.

10:22.

Time was of the essence, and yet time meant nothing at all. All that mattered now were her memories. They rolled in on the fog that now consumed her. Scenes of Ashley's life began to play over and over in her mind. . . .

A little girl, happy, carefree—running across a field, chasing butterflies. A lovely teenager, pressed timidly in the corner at a high school dance. A giddy college student, thanking her father for the plane tickes to Vienna, where she could finally experience the music she loved first-hand. A nervous young woman in a doctor's waiting room, wringing her hands, bracing herself for the worst. . .

Help me! her heart cried out, lips remaining motionless.

She stared at a vase of yellow roses, a final gift from her mother.

Help me! she cried, a little girl once again. This time she was standing in the backyard, facing a chain link fence, clutching a fistful of Mama's yellow roses from the garden. On the other side of the fence, just a step away. . .a Rottweiler, teeth extended, barking his head off. His breath was hot in her face.

"It's okay, Ashley!" Mama's tender voice spoke. She was nearby.

She could make it right. Mama could make anything right.

But Mama wasn't here either. Even she hadn't been allowed to be here at the end. A final embrace, and she had disappeared into the hallway half an hour before. All that remained were the roses—a parting gift, an emblem.

"The yellow rose of Texas." That's what Daddy had always called her. But Daddy was gone, himself a victim of cancer's ugly blight. The fog enveloped her again, and she gave herself over to it.

Dreams. Dreams.

All she had were her dreams.

From across the room, the television droned on. A new president was about to be inaugurated—the first female president in the history of the United States—Charlotte Tinsdale. Ashley had voted for her, even helped out at party headquarters during the election year. But what good would that do now? She wouldn't even live to see her take the oath of office. Even that dream was being ripped away.

"Do you need any help in here?" A loud male voice rang out suddenly, shattering the silence in the room.

Daddy?

No, it wasn't Daddy. But the young doctor's voice had shocked a very groggy Ashley back to reality—at least to some extent. Had he always been here, or had he just come in? Was he here to help her? She tried, through the fog, to get a clear picture of him. He looked young, unfamiliar. Yet there was something about those deep green eyes. He peered down at her, almost curiously, it seemed. There was an anxiety there, something she could easily relate to, despite her condition.

Help me!

Surely Ashley's eyes conveyed her terror. Didn't he realize she wanted out of here? How could she get him to stop the IV?

"Nah, I don't need any help. It's just a matter of time," the nurse said, yawning impatiently. "The machine's set to hit Phase Two in just about three minutes."

Phase Two? Ah yes, the transition from soothing tranquilizer to lethal drip. . .

God?!?! Help me!

God? Was there a God? Why, she hadn't thought about Him in years. Why was it so important now? Was He there, watching? Surely not! How could a loving God let something like this happen? But was He loving, or was He. . .angry? Ashley began to tremble uncontrollably with another terrible memory. . . .

She was only four at the time, but to this day she could still hear the vicious words of her Aunt Sharon, bony finger shaking violently in her face: *"God doesn't deal very kindly with little liars like you, Ashley Cooper. He's got a punishment for you worse than I could ever give with this switch. You'll burn in hell for all eternity. You just wait and see."*

Was it true? Was God really out to get her? Was He up there with Aunt Sharon, laughing, jeering? Worse yet—was she about to meet Him face-to-face? Or was she really on her way to an eternal hell? *No! Please, no!*

Drip, drip, drip. . .

The IV began to pick up speed now, along with the beating of her heart.

Don't touch me! She tried to scream.

Nothing.

Her heart was really going to town now, drugs or no drugs. The young man must have noticed. He glanced at the monitor, obviously aware of the increased rate of her heartbeat.

What was he going to do? The unfamiliar face leaned over her, staring intently into her eyes. Ashley closed them tightly, feeling the pull of the poison drawing her in.

Suddenly it didn't matter anymore. Nothing mattered. Ashley closed her eyes, releasing herself to the pull of the medication. She was on her way to Vienna, symphony playing madly. She was slipping. . . .

It was almost over now, almost over. . . .

Two

Aaron Landers flipped nervously through the young woman's chart. The smell of death was already in the room, and it left him nauseated.

"Attending physician?" He spoke the words carefully, staring intently at the nurse. The young doctor knew the answer, even before it came. Who else could it be?

"Old Doc Bishop. Do you know him?"

Know him? Who didn't? Bishop had instructed a mandatory course in euthanasia during his last semester in med school. "Death with Dignity." That's what it had been called. It was a course he would never forget. It left a lasting impression. In fact, it was the very reason he. . . Well, no time to think about that right now.

"Only by reputation," he said.

"Yeah, well—he's got quite a reputation," the nurse muttered.

"Fill me in. I'm new here." Aaron spoke hastily. That much was true.

"He, uh. . .he always hates to be here at the end," the nurse explained—a little too carefully. "New or not—I'm sure you've heard how the old guy is. Scared to death of death."

Odd answer. Aaron glanced at his watch quickly.

10:24. Where was Doc Bishop? According to Ashley Cooper's chart, he was supposed to be here—required to be here.

21

"What about you?" Aaron asked. "You look like you could use a break."

The nurse shrugged. "Doesn't bother me anymore. . . . Besides, someone has to be here to fill in the time on the death certificate. He's already signed it."

Waiting for someone to die. It was an odd feeling—made this young doctor extremely uneasy. Surely there was more to medicine than this. . . .

"You must be tired," he argued, glancing at his watch again. 10:25.

"Why don't you slip down to the nurses' lounge?" he urged her. "I'll stay here until she passes."

"I don't know. . . ," the nurse answered with a shrug.

"Ah, come on. I'll cover for you," he argued, dropping into the chair next to the bed.

His eyes turned instinctively to the young woman in the bed. Less than a minute now. . .

"Okay, but it's your neck if I get caught. . . ." The words he had been waiting for.

"Here," Aaron said, reaching for the death certificate. "Let me have that. I'll fill in the time when it comes."

"Whatever."

The nurse reluctantly handed him the piece of paper she had held in her tight grasp and headed for the door.

"Thanks."

Aaron breathed a sigh of relief, approaching the bed. Leaning down, he gazed into Ashley Cooper's helpless green eyes. Terror had long since been replaced with resolve. She was dying. And he was here to. . .

Why was he here again?

"There must be something you can do!" They were his own words, words he had spoken on a night over three years ago—a night that would haunt him, and provoke him. . . .

"Do something! Don't just stand there!" The words of his sister, frantic, pleading, coaxing through the tears.

But stand he did, over the lifeless bodies of his mother and father, already cold—innocent victims of a senseless robbery turned murder. There was nothing he or anyone else could do. . . . So why did he feel so guilty?

"You were supposed to be there! This wouldn't have happened if you. . ."

He hadn't been there. A rushed phone call from the hospital had conveyed the message. He was too busy to come to dinner. He was too busy. . .too busy. . . .

"Do something!"

The death machine clicked to its next phase, startling Aaron back to reality. He looked down into the helpless face of Ashley Cooper, resolve building.

"Do something," he whispered.

Aaron Landers was completely unprepared for the adrenaline rush that gripped him as he reached over the bed and unplugged it. Nothing had prepared him for a moment such as this, though his heart urged him on with every frantic beat. He quickly checked Ashley Cooper's pulse, glancing at the clock on the wall.

10:27.

She was almost gone. How much of the deadly poison had already entered her bloodstream? Was he too late?

"It's your neck if I get caught!" Nurse Gina Evans had spoken the words hesitantly before leaving her post. She didn't know the young doctor, probably new on staff, but he looked honest enough. Besides, if anyone on staff deserved a break, she did.

There was a huge turnover in this department, not that she had anything to do with that. It was a tough gig. Killing people didn't come naturally for those in the medical profession. If she ever doubted that, all she had to do was look at old Doc Bishop. He was all the proof anyone would ever need.

THREE

Dr. Blaine Bishop took a final swallow of the stale coffee and glanced at his watch.

10:26. Probably not yet. He yawned, leaning back in the cafeteria chair. It wobbled, nearly toppling over backward onto the stark white linoleum floor.

"That'll wake you up." A cute nurse giggled as she walked by.

Blaine felt his face redden, glancing only momentarily into her clear blue eyes. They twinkled back her merriment. How embarrassing. Now, how to turn this thing around. . .

He cleared his throat and tried to act as if nothing out of the ordinary had occurred. "Would you like to have a seat?" he asked the pretty blond, gesturing to the seat next to him.

She shook her head. "No thanks. I'm in a hurry."

"Right. Sure," came his frustrated response. Blaine forced a smile, trying not to let her reaction hurt his feelings. Of course she didn't want to sit with him. She was young, pretty. . . He was, well, more mature, and certainly not good-looking enough to suit the likes of her. Besides, his position at the hospital hardly commanded respect from the others on staff.

"Your loss," he mumbled to himself, glaring up at her as she made her way to the lunch counter.

He had grown used to the rejection, though it still stabbed at him when he least expected it. The young woman went on, unaware of his thoughts or words, and Blaine settled back against the chair once again, taking another look at his watch.

10:28. Was this day never going to end? He reached down with his fork, diving it into the stiff slice of apple pie, still cold from the serving line.

"Ugh!" It was almost as stale as the coffee. What did it matter? Even his favorite foods left a bitter taste in his mouth these days. Nothing seemed to be able to drive it away.

Suddenly he heard it, as clearly as anything he had ever heard spoken in his life. *"Murderer!"* Blaine turned sharply, staring at the young nurse. A mixture of fear and anger rose up within him. Who did she think she was? What right did she have? . . .

"Murderer!" He heard it again. And yet it couldn't have been the nurse. She was oblivious to his stares, deep in conversation with a fellow worker.

But surely he wasn't imagining things. Blaine had heard her shout out the word—the same ugly word that haunted him night after night when sleep wouldn't come—the convicting word that described the truth of who he was, what he was.

"Murderer!"

No! Put it out of your mind, Blaine. Forget it.

Still trembling, the weary doctor closed his eyes, trying to free himself from the guilt associated with that word. It haunted him— like a fresh carcass refusing burial, it followed him wherever he went. No, this was certainly not the first time it had happened. Such moments were coming all too closely these days. Best to try and forget it altogether.

Blaine attempted to relax, to push all of the day's events firmly behind him.

Get a grip, Man.

Yes, that was better. Slow deep breaths always seemed to help. He let his mind drift off to a place far away, a place with peaceful ocean waves lapping the shoreline, children running merrily along the beach. A place where friends and family came together to forget the cares of the world.

Cares of the world. . .

Blaine sighed deeply. Some cares were far too pressing to forget. Even now he was supposed to be somewhere else, not lounging in the hospital cafeteria, chasing nightmares. He didn't even need to be daydreaming about pretty nurses. What Blaine needed was a place to rest, to think—or rather not to think. The turmoil in his life over the last few months had left him feeling more than a little unsettled.

A respected surgeon for nearly thirty-four years, Dr. Blaine Bishop was certain that his future was written in stone at Houston's famous Mercy Hospital, buried deep in the heart of the world-famous medical center. Apparently the hospital administrators had other ideas. There was an overabundance of surgeons on staff, or so he had been told six months ago. Besides, they had a better plan. . . .

Ironically, their decision came just three days after the new law went into effect. It was then that he received the news that would forever change his life, his goals, his direction. Not that change was bad, necessarily. It's just that this was a pretty drastic change.

"A raise, Blaine! A new position!"

He should have been happy, proud—or so they all said. After all, he had been chosen to head up a brand-new wing of the hospital, "Crossings." It sounded respectable enough.

Crossings.

"Think of it, Man! We're headed off into uncharted waters! And whom do they ask to steer the ship? Whom, I ask you? Blaine Bishop!"

Crossings.

"This wing will change the direction of medicine in this city."

He knew it was true. But still—there was something about the name that bothered him, something that he couldn't quite reconcile. . . .

Crossings. A fancy name for death.

What had started out as "mercy" killing had quickly evolved into something far more sinister. For those in compromised physical or mental health, the so-called "right" to die had quickly become the "duty" to die. The result? Hospitals across the country had been forced to equip themselves for the inevitable—the continual, ever-present, ongoing process of elimination.

Elimination.

Of course, they didn't call it that. After all, even when you took your dog to the vet, they called it "being put to sleep." A common courtesy.

A mask.

So the name "Crossings" was concocted. It seemed so reasonable, so practical. Putting people to sleep. It was an odd job, but someone had to do it. Blaine had taken on the title of Obitiatrist— a doctor who specializes in killing his patients. Not a flattering designation, or one he was terribly proud of, but something he had certainly become an expert in. Providing a kinder, gentler death was the service he performed. It was all so. . .antiseptic.

Gone were the days of bioethics discussions. No more questions about physician-assisted suicide versus palliative care. Gone were the complaints against HMOs. Even self-deliverance was becoming a thing of the past. Far different discussions were taking place these days.

"Blaine! Help me! Help me!"

He sat up in the chair, looking about. No one. This voice was clearly from his past.

"How can I? We've tried everything! Don't you know that? Don't you trust me? What else do you want me to do? . . ." his only answer.

But the voice lingered, hung on the one word that bothered him the most. . .

"Help! . . ."

He had to shake himself out of it. There was no use dwelling on the past. Blaine looked at his watch again.

10:31. Up in room 244, a young woman was dying. Perhaps she was already gone. . . .

No, he mustn't think about that right now. He had left Ashley Cooper in good hands. Nurse Gina Evans had been through this process time and time again over the last six months. She knew her stuff. She also knew he hated to be there at the end.

They had an understanding. He would administer the "medication," make sure the machine was set up properly. She would wait it out. And for her added effort, a crisp fifty-dollar bill each time.

"No problem," he mumbled. At least there shouldn't have been. But, unlike many of his contemporaries, Blaine Bishop had taken the Hippocratic oath thirty-four years ago—long before the medical community had passed laws eliminating the "need" for it. He was from the old school.

The oath had served its purpose in its time. Or so they had said. It had long since been replaced with a new "Oath of Duty"— "Society has an obligation to rid itself of defective individuals, regardless of their age, race, or religious convictions. . . ."

Blaine was torn over the issue. He was supposed to be saving lives, not taking them. The wrestling match going on in his mind was evidence of that. But what choice did he have? Besides, they were hardly "lives" that he was taking, now were they?

No. They were terminal, most of them. The others were indigent, mentally unbalanced, or defective in one way or another. They were incapable of contributing to society. In other words, they were hardly worth saving. It was justifiable, not that he had anything to say about it, anyway. Blaine played no part in deciding who would enter Crossings. He just dealt with the "patients" as they came through.

Of course, there was some guilt about the others—the ones who weren't really terminal. The ones who, once typed and matched, met the criteria as organ donors. And, of course, there was also a twinge of guilt about the money he had taken under the table from children who had simply grown weary of caring for their aging parents. "Diagnosing" and eliminating the otherwise healthy elderly had caused him a few sleepless nights—but only a few. The financial incentives had been worth it.

One more glance at the watch.

10:32. There. It was surely over by now. Blaine stood, stretching, preparing himself for the long walk back to room 244 where

Nurse Evans would be waiting. His eyes traveled up to the sign above the door—Mercy Hospital Cares About Its Patients, it read in multicolored brilliance. Another guilty reminder.

Are they ever going to take that thing down? he wondered. Blaine took one last lingering look at the pretty blond before leaving. "Too bad," he mumbled, turning to leave the comfort of the cafeteria.

Click, click, click.

His shoes made a hollow, rhythmic sound as he forced his way down the long, vacant corridor. How strangely empty the hospital seemed today.

"There must be something you can do!" The voice riveted him again.

What?! What?! There was nothing he could do—now or then. . . . So why the overwhelming guilt, the feeling of. . .

Helplessness. . .

He was all alone. No, thank God, he wasn't. Here was a friendly face. James Hall, neurologist, approached with a smile.

"Hello, Blaine."

"Hello, yourself," he answered with a nod.

Click, click, click.

A hollow echo. The two passed without another word. And then, just as he was almost out of earshot, it came again. *"Murderer!"* Blaine turned back to face the other doctor. Who did he think he was, anyway? *"Murderer!"* There it was again! Blaine wasn't losing his mind.

Or was he? Dr. Hall continued in the opposite direction, oblivious to his frightened stares. Blaine fought to catch his breath, afraid for a moment that he might pass out. This had to stop.

He cringed as he turned to enter the familiar hall. The smell of death was everywhere. Even the best of cleaning chemicals couldn't erase the nauseating aroma from this wing of the hospital. Up ahead Nurse Evans stood at the nurses' station, back turned toward him as he approached.

"Hey, what are you doing out here?" Dr. Bishop whispered nervously.

Gina turned to face him, her face a little paler than usual. "Oh, uh—it's all. . .all over."

"So soon? Where's the death certificate?"

Gina fumbled around in the large pockets of her nursing uniform but came up empty. "I, uh, must have left it in the room. It's filled out and ready."

Blaine watched as she sprinted toward the room. How odd. She was usually so careful about such things.

Nurse Gina Evans trembled as she turned toward the room where Ashley Cooper's near-lifeless body lay just moments ago. What was Dr. Bishop doing back this soon?

This was going to be Gina's undoing, her ruin. And it couldn't have come at a worse time. A single mother with two teenage sons, she was barely making ends meet on her meager salary. That's why Blaine Bishop's money under the table had been a welcome addition.

But now she was about to lose it all—the money, the job, everything. In seconds he would know that she had left her post before the job was complete, before. . .

Gina shook uncontrollably as she rounded the door and entered room 244.

Empty.

Clean.

No way! How did he do that?

She breathed a deep sigh of relief, content in the fact that she had just been granted a reprieve. She would have to remember to thank the young doctor later. He sure knew how to clean up after himself. No one had ever turned a room that quickly. He was a miracle worker.

But where was the death certificate? *Ah ha!*

She snatched it from the bedside tray and sprinted back to the doctor's side, pressing it into his outstretched hand.

"Here it is," she said, more than a little out of breath.

"Time of death. . ." He ran his finger down the page until he came to the spot he had been looking for. "10:28?"

Gina's heart skipped a beat, anticipating his response.

"10:28?" he repeated, looking down at his watch.

She nodded numbly, waiting, worrying.

"We made good time with this one," Dr. Bishop said, smiling broadly. He reached out to pat her on the shoulder. "Good girl. There may be an extra fifty in this one for you."

She met the touch with a mixture of fear and relief. "Thanks, Dr. Bishop," she said, trying to steady her breathing.

"No. Thank you, Gina. As usual, I couldn't have done it without you."

"No problem," she whispered, turning the other way.

Her heart still pounding in her ears, Gina headed into another room, ready to face another in the endless line of patients.

Aaron Landers rapidly pushed the stretcher that held Ashley Cooper's near-lifeless body toward the east exit of the hospital. His guise as a medical student had worked once again. The whole thing had gone off without a hitch—at least so far.

Aaron carefully tightened the sheet over Ashley's head. No one would be any the wiser. Folks had grown accustomed to seeing bodies transported to and fro in this department. That's what Crossings was all about.

There. He had made it. The exit was in sight. Here he was to make the transfer into the waiting ambulance. Everything had been prearranged, each detail carefully orchestrated.

A woman jumped from the front of the ambulance to assist him, eyes darting about nervously.

"This her?" she asked in hushed whisper.

"No. I decided to hold out for a blond," he answered with a grin.

"Very funny."

Quickly, yet ever so quietly, they placed Ashley Cooper in the rear of the vehicle. Aaron jumped in, taking his usual place behind the wheel.

"Ready?" he asked.

"Ready as I'll ever be," came the woman's swift reply.

Aaron breathed a huge sigh of relief, realizing for the first time that he was trembling. "What's the matter, Aaron?" he whispered to himself. "Losing your touch?"

Nah. In fact, Aaron Landers was becoming such a pro at this that he just might work up the courage to try his hand at an acting career in Hollywood when this stint was over.

On the other side of the country, with millions of eyes looking on, Charlotte Tinsdale raised a trembling right hand to take the most important oath of her life. It was a day that would forever change the course of American history.

FOUR

Push, Coral, push!"

The young mother-to-be heard the obstetrician's words but was already one step ahead of him. Before his final word was spoken, Baby Jamie made his entrance into the world, squealing with anticipation.

"It's a boy," a nurse said anxiously, glancing only for a moment in Coral's direction.

A boy. Her husband, Jacob, had been right all along.

"Pink or blue?" Coral asked, holding up a wallpaper sample.

"Blue."

"I like pink."

"But what if it's a boy?" Jacob had tried to argue. "No son of mine is going to grow up with pink flowers on his bedroom wall. What about this one with the baseball bats?"

They had compromised on the green.

"I love you, Babe." Jacob's tender voice snapped her back to reality.

"Love you, too," she whispered, suddenly feeling the exhaustion plow her down like a freight train. Coral Summerlin breathed a huge sigh of relief, dropping back onto the bed, hand still tightly gripping her husband's. Beads of sweat poured over her eyebrows into her eyes, stinging. She reached up to wipe them, noticing for the first time how hard she was shaking. It was probably as much from the cold of the sterile room as from exhaustion.

Her hand slowed as it brushed away the sweat, now mingled with a tear. Finally, after twenty-six long hours of labor, it was over.

"Time?" the pediatrician asked.

Coral looked up at the large clock on the wall just as the nurse spoke the words: "10:28 A.M." She whispered in sync.

"All right, note that." His voice sounded peculiar, worried.

"Is everything okay?" Coral asked quietly. Her husband, Jacob, stood next to her, squeezing her hand. It was a comforting squeeze, but something in his grip stirred concern. He shrugged, reaching down to whisper in her ear, "You know how they are. They take everything so seriously."

"Go see. Please," she urged him.

He turned toward the doctors and nurses, nodding. They were more than a little preoccupied with the newborn.

"Tina Marie. What do you think of that name, Jacob? Tina Marie?"

"I think he's gonna feel pretty dumb walking around with a name like that."

"No, really, Honey. . ."

"Really!"

"Apgar?" the doctor's voice jolted her back once again.

"Let me have a look at that. . . ."

"Did you check the? . . ."

No, something was certainly not right here. What was that look on Jacob's face? Did he know something that she didn't?

The obstetrician continued on with his work, placing necessary stitches. Coral watched his eyes drift to the area where the newborn lay. Her eyes followed his, anxious, worried.

Across the room there was now a strained hush. Shouldn't someone be talking, or laughing—or something? Coral glanced to her left where the pediatrician was analyzing the baby, her baby. How she longed to lay eyes on him! She could hardly wait.

But she must wait. He must be weighed, measured. . .

"James Daniel, if it's a boy," Coral had finally agreed. *"But only if we can call him Jamie."*

"Jamie?" Jacob had tried to argue. "Isn't that a girl's name?"

Jamie. . . she mouthed the word silently now.

Why were the nurses whispering? Why wasn't anyone looking her in the eye?

"Can I see him?" Coral asked, smiling, arms extended.

She had dreamed of this moment—the touch of the newborn's skin, the sweet smell of talcum powder, the kisses she would scatter all over his tiny forehead. . . .

Jamie! Jamie!

"Uh, just a minute, Coral," pediatrician Kevin Norwood stammered.

Was there a problem? Coral's heart began to race. Something must be wrong with the baby. Anxiously her eyes sought out Jacob's. He looked tense, strained. But he was still forcing a smile.

"What's going on?" she asked, after a moment or two of silence. It was impossible not to notice the panic-stricken look the nurse shot at the pediatrician.

"It's, uh. . ."

Please God! Don't let me lose this baby! Not Jamie, too!

Two previous miscarriages had all but caused her to stop hoping she would ever have a child. To carry this one all these months only to lose him would be. . .

No, she wouldn't let herself think like that. Memories rose like an ocean wave, overtaking her. . . .

"If it's a boy, promise me you won't dress him in ruffles and lace," Jacob had argued. *"I can't stand that. And no dolls."*

"I promise," Coral had agreed. *"And if it's a girl, she'll have ballet lessons and play the piano. I always wanted to learn how to play the piano."*

The wave settled. Coral looked into Jacob's eyes. He was frightened. There was no hiding it now.

"Just say it," Jacob spoke insistently to the doctors.

Whatever it is, she whispered inside herself, *we can take it.*

"Down's syndrome."

The words cut like a knife. Down's syndrome? That was impossible. This wasn't a high-risk pregnancy. Coral was only in her mid-thirties. Why in the world would she have given birth to a Down's syndrome baby? "There must be some mistake," she stammered, a tear working its way down her flushed cheek. "Let me see him."

Reluctantly the nurse handed the baby over. It was true. The tiny, beautiful, round face stared up at her.

"Down's syndrome," she whispered, running her finger across the precious features. His eyes were large and as black as a cavern. His forehead, high and flat, was a sign that their diagnosis was, indeed, correct.

"You were absolutely perfect when you were born. That's why we chose you!" They were her own mother's words, an assurance that her adoption had granted her the status of a real daughter, despite a heart condition at birth.

"But. . ."

"No buts!" Coral's mother had said, hugging her tight. *"You were exactly what we wanted!"*

It had been enough to convince a young, insecure preteen. And it was enough to assure her now. Jamie was no accident. His "condition" didn't matter. They would get through it, somehow. This was her child, her son.

"You're beautiful, Jamie," she whispered, unable to stop the flow of tears that were falling from her cheek onto his.

Coral looked up at Jacob. The tears were streaming down his face, too. Was he happy, sad? . . . It was hard to tell. The mixture of emotions sweeping Coral was dizzying. Surely Jacob was just as confused.

"I love you," he whispered, leaning down to plant a kiss on Coral's forehead.

"I love you back," she responded, watching as Jacob gently ran his finger across Jamie's misshaped brow.

Their smile connected them. It was magical.

Conversation between the doctors was growing heated.

"Didn't you do an amniocentesis?" the pediatrician demanded, the strain on his face apparent.

"We tried," Coral's obstetrician, James Milliken, responded defiantly. "It was impossible. The placenta was covering the abdomen. We couldn't get the needle through it into the amniotic fluid."

That much was true. Coral remembered the obstetrician's attempts. Try after painful try had resulted in nothing but frustration. He had finally given up, convinced that Coral's pregnancy was moving along beautifully with or without an amniocentesis.

"I wasn't really worried about chromosomal abnormalities or genetic defects. We were just trying to hang on to this baby to term. She had lost two in less than a year." He tried to explain, words futile.

"You know the law," Dr. Norwood said, reaching for the baby. "They can take your license for this—at the very least."

"I, uh. . ." Dr. Milliken stammered, eyes suddenly looking glassy. "It couldn't be helped. And I've got the documents to prove it. I did everything I could."

The pediatrician reached for Baby Jamie. Coral's grip grew tighter, not yet ready to give him up. "What are you doing?"

"I need to take him, Mrs. Summerlin." His agitation was evident.

"But. . ."

"We'll take good care of him. Now don't you worry!" the nurse said, patting her arm.

Coral reluctantly placed her son into the waiting arms of the pediatrician, who turned to leave the room. She had no sooner done so, than the trembling began. Overwhelmed with fear, she suddenly realized what she had just done. She had just handed her son over to. . .

"Where are you taking him?" she quizzed, attempting to sit up.

"Lie down, Honey," the nurse said, placing a firm hand on her shoulder.

"Bring him back," the possessive new mother called out, feeling her blood pressure begin to mount.

"Coral, I'll be in to talk with you in just a few minutes," the pediatrician said abruptly.

"Where are they taking him?" Jacob asked, the anger in his voice evident.

"We really have no choice in cases like this," Dr. Milliken whispered hoarsely.

"Cases like what?" Coral demanded. What in the world was he talking about?

"Defective children."

"Defective?" Jacob argued. "That's crazy."

"Crazy or not, it's the law."

"I don't know what you're talking about," Coral argued. "Where is he taking my baby?"

Dead silence.

"Please. You have to tell me," Coral begged, tears rolling down her cheek.

"He's going to the Crossings nursery."

"Crossings?" Jacob stammered. "What in the world is that—some kind of an intensive care unit?"

Dr. Milliken shook his head, and Coral's heart began to race uncontrollably.

"I could have saved you all of this trouble if the amniocentesis had worked. We could have performed a late-term abortion—even taken care of it here today. There's no controversy surrounding partial-birth anymore. . . ."

"No!" Coral cried out. "I don't believe in abortion!"

She sought out Jacob's face anxiously. He was shaking his head violently.

"You would have had no choice in the matter, Honey," the nurse said, coming to the doctor's defense. "Just like you have no choice now. It's the law. We have an obligation to rid society of defective children. It's a part of our calling as medical personnel."

"What are you saying?"

"I don't know how I can make this any plainer, Coral," Dr. Milliken stated simply, dropping into a chair next to the bed.

"Your son is defective. They've taken him to Crossings. You've got thirty days to prepare, and then they'll euthanize him."

"W–what?!"

"Over my dead body!" Jacob stated, heading for the door.

"You don't understand, Jacob. It's the law."

The law?

Coral turned to look at him, clutching at his hand. She was now shaking uncontrollably. The room had become a morgue.

"No!"

First the horror of realizing their child was born somewhat less than perfect and now this!

"They can't do that!" she shouted. "Who do these people think they are—God?!"

"Careful!"

Aaron Landers heard the woman's frantic words and hit the brakes quickly. The vehicle took a sharp turn, narrowly avoiding the curb.

"Can't you drive any faster?!" They were his own words from three years ago—the infamous night—the night that had changed everything. He was seated in the back of the ambulance that carried his parents' lifeless bodies to Mercy Hospital in Houston's busy medical center, his sister crumpled in an emotional heap beside him.

"Do something! Do something!" she had pleaded.

"But. . .they're already gone. . . ."

Everything else was a blur.

But that was then. . .not now. Gaining control of the vehicle, Aaron looked back at his patient.

"Hang on, Ashley," he whispered, reaching for her lifeless hand. "Hang on!"

"I do," Charlotte Tinsdale said, putting her trembling hand down.

There. That wasn't so tough. She had made it through with

barely a stumbling word, in fact. She looked out over the crowd anxiously, searching for a friendly face.

It wasn't every day that one became the first female president in the history of the United States.

FIVE

Well, I never thought I'd live to see the day," old Molly Gilbert muttered, staring at the television set. "A female president! As I live and breathe! Not that I'll be living and breathing much longer. . ."

"Oh, pooh!" her sister Hannah exclaimed, reaching over to turn off the television. "You just get yourself so worked up, Molly Gilbert!"

"That's only because there's so much to get worked up about!" Sixty-seven-year-old Molly mumbled, wringing her hands. "So much. . .so much!"

"What now?" Hannah asked, already knowing the answer. She had Molly's speech memorized perfectly. She could practically recite it from memory.

"You know perfectly well what," Molly answered angrily. "It's just a matter of time before they cart me off."

"Molly. Stop it."

"I wouldn't expect you to understand. You're only sixty-three. You've still got some time before they haul you in."

"Stop it, Molly." Hannah answered her sister with the usual cheery smile.

"This is serious."

"I know it," Hannah answered, her smile fading only slightly. "I just like to look on the bright side, that's all. Don't be such a worrywart! Have some faith."

"Faith? I'm supposed to have faith?" Molly's stubborn streak faded, her chin beginning its usual quiver. Hannah couldn't help but melt like butter.

It was a legitimate question, all things considered. There wasn't much for an older person to be encouraged about these days. This Hannah knew all too well. Even a trip to the doctor's office could result in devastating consequences.

But Hannah seemed to have a knack for seeing beyond the situation. She was prepared, one way or the other. Whether she lived twenty years or twenty minutes, she was going to make the best of it. She was determined to take the high road.

Molly, on the other hand. . .

Molly was the oldest and, consequently, at the greatest risk. This was an undeniable fact—a fact Hannah was reminded of every minute of every day. Her sister was in perfect health, though you wouldn't know it by all of her moaning and groaning. Ever since the inception of Duty to Die, Molly had driven herself into a frenzied state of worry and despair, preparing herself for what looked like the inevitable. But now, with a new president in office, things might very well be looking up.

"It's not bad enough I've got to deal with this rheumatism day and night. . . ," the older sister mumbled, depression evident.

"You don't have rheumatism, Molly," Hannah said firmly. "And you know it."

She didn't seem to know it.

"I'm aching all over. But how can I go to a doctor?" Molly argued. "You know what will happen. . . ."

"Sister, please. . ." Hannah tried to respond, but it was useless.

The law was terrible, to be sure, but it didn't make any sense to sit around moping all day like Molly seemed content to do. There was so much living yet to be done—flowers to be planted, neighbors to be visited, joys to be discovered. In all of the years the two sisters had spent together in this old, wood-framed house on the outskirts of downtown Houston, there was simply no time so precious as the present.

"Come with me to the market," Hannah said, reaching for her jacket. "I feel like a walk."

"It's too cold out. I'll catch my death. . . ."

"Or maybe get hit by a bus," Hannah mumbled under her breath.

"That wasn't funny. And for your information, they said on the news that we're under a smog alert today. They'll have to cart me off in an ambulance if I take one step out that door on a day like this."

"Look here, Sister," Hannah said firmly, "You're entirely too consumed with worry. You've got to get out more, got to live—while there's still time."

"Time? Who has time?" Molly muttered. "Besides, I'm living—the only way I know how."

"Not much of a life—preparing to die!" Hannah argued. "Now come on. I'm not going to wait all day."

"Are you going to wear that purple hat with the flowers again?" Molly asked smugly.

"Yes." Hannah plopped it on her head. "Why?"

"Hmph!" Molly picked up the newspaper, pretending to read. "I'm not going."

"Suit yourself." Hannah swung the door wide, stepping out into the afternoon sun. "I'm on my way!"

She pulled the door shut behind her, shaking her head as it pulled to. How could she make her sister understand? Life was precious. It was for the living!

But what a life. Molly's loud complaining was as clear as a bell, even from behind the closed door. So this was how it was going to be—again. Day in and day out, the same old story.

"I won't let you stop me, Molly Gilbert!" Hannah muttered under her breath. "I won't!"

She took a deep breath, letting the breeze consume her. Everything was suddenly fresh again. Hope was in the air. It was wonderful to be alive, simply wonderful!

"Afternoon, Delia!" she hollered, waving to a neighbor lady.

"Afternoon. . . ," came the ragged response.

This aging neighborhood was filled with people almost as old as the homes that housed them. The skyscrapers of Houston loomed to the right, less than a mile away. They cast an ominous shadow over the neighborhood, causing many of its occupants to stay indoors far more than they should. They were depressed, most of them—without any hope. Just blocks away, life was moving at an alarmingly rapid pace. But here in this little neighborhood, the contrast was very real. It was as if the city itself held these people captive, tight in its grip.

Well, Hannah was going to see to it that that changed. She had made it her mission to give these folks something to live for. She would, at the very least, offer a smile and a wave. And joy. . . She would offer them joy. After all, she had plenty to spare.

With a skip in her step, she moved toward the market.

Drip, Drip, Drip!

Ashley Cooper pulled frantically at the IV in her arm, the nightmare continuing on. She was moving fast, fast, faster. . . .

SIX

Drive faster! Drive faster!"

The words pressed Aaron Landers ever onward as he drove like a madman away from Mercy Hospital.

"Drive faster!" They were today's voices—and voices from the past, always present, unrelenting. . .

"Do something!" The voice of his sister, shrill, terrified.

Would she ever forgive him? Could she ever forgive him?

Shannon Carpenter waited anxiously for the results of the home pregnancy test, counting down the seconds as if they were hours.

Blue—pregnant. White—not pregnant. Blue—pregnant. White—not pregnant.

She gripped the white plastic test-case, hands shaking uncontrollably. She stared, eyes focused, unblinking. Her heart was pounding in her ears, causing her to feel faint. What would it be?

The answer came quickly—a definitive blue streak.

Positive.

A mixture of happiness and fear shot through her, forcing her knees to buckle. Uncontrollable tears began to flow. She took a seat on the couch, a new French import, catching her breath. Thirty-three-year-old Shannon should have been thrilled, but she knew what this news meant. It meant that her life would never be the same. Decisions would have to be made—and quickly. Decisions, choices. . .

Choices.

Did she have any, really?

Shannon stared down at the playpen to her right where her young toddler, Zachary, played happily. Six-year-old daughter Veronica was in school, probably having the time of her life. Neither of them could possibly understand the confusion of this moment.

And Frank, her husband of nine years, how would he take this news—this wonderful, terrible news? No doubt his reaction would leave something to be desired. Frank was going through so much at work already. They hardly got to see each other anymore, now that his law firm had taken on its latest client—an important government official working closely with the Duty to Die legislators.

Duty to Die. Hmmm. She shuddered, realizing how close to home this law had suddenly struck.

"Do something!"

But what could be done? To her right the big-screen television was blaring. The inauguration. She had planned to watch it, but it seemed to be the farthest thing from her mind now. Charlotte Tinsdale's smiling face captivated her for a moment, drawing her away from the situation momentarily.

A female president. The first one ever. What would that mean for the country? What would that mean for her? Would the new law remain intact? Would former President Klingerman's zeal for Duty to Die still reverberate as loudly through the lips of this woman. . .this widow?

Funny. Up until now, Shannon might have sided with Frank and the others who had written the law. It had all seemed so sensible. At least until today. But now, for the first time, she suddenly found herself on the opposite side of the fence—and it was an awkward place to be.

Shannon stared, captivated, at the television, watching Charlotte Tinsdale. Two young boys stood at her side. Her sons looked to be in their early teens, maybe a little younger—she couldn't tell.

Surely, if this woman had children, two children, she would understand the predicament Shannon now found herself in.

Well, no time to worry about that right now. She had to talk to Frank. Shannon picked up the phone to dial his number at work. She pushed a wisp of bleached-blond hair back behind her ear as she hugged the phone close. She wasn't blond by choice. Frank preferred it that way, and whatever Frank wanted, Frank usually got.

"Carpenter and Morris," the familiar voice came on the line.

"Frank Carpenter, please," she stammered.

"Oh, I'm sorry, Mrs. Carpenter. He's not in right now. He's in a meeting across town."

"Any idea when he'll be back?" Shannon asked anxiously.

"No idea. Sorry. Could I take a message?"

Tears began to stream down Shannon's face. She fought to keep her voice from shaking. "No."

"You might try him on his mobile," the voice continued, ever businesslike.

"Thank you," she whispered, dropping the phone back into the socket.

She gazed around the quiet room helplessly. If only there were someone to talk to, someone to confide in. A scratch on the back door distracted her for a moment.

"Okay, Gilligan, I'll let you in." She opened the door to welcome the furry puppy, just nine weeks old yesterday. "What do you want, Fella? Are you hungry? I just fed you, didn't I?"

Did she? She couldn't remember. Well, a little more food wouldn't hurt, one way or the other.

Shannon reached up to grab the bag of dog food from the top of the refrigerator. She had been keeping it there ever since two-year-old Zachary had discovered it and thought it was yummy. She poured a little into Gilligan's bowl, looking down at him with a smile as he dove into it. It provided a nice distraction—for a moment.

Shannon glanced at her watch. . .10:42. She hated to disturb

Frank in his meeting, but she must speak to him. How could she wait here alone, with no one to talk to, no one to advise her? But no, she couldn't bother him. . . .

She dropped down onto the couch, eyes closed, deep in thought. Everything she and Frank had worked so hard for—their lovely home in prestigious River Oaks, their new Lexus, everything could be lost over this.

"Do something!"

The words came again, along with a flashing chill. They shot through her like a bolt of lightning, bringing guilt and fear. The faces of her parents were all she could see.

"No!" she found herself shouting.

"I should have been there. I should have. . ."

"There's nothing anyone could have done." Her brother's words.

Her brother.

Why would she think of him now, in the middle of all of this? They had hardly spoken since that awful night.

No. He was the last person she would turn to.

Ashley Cooper cried out in agony as the gruesome nightmare continued.

Drip, drip, drip!

It was unending, agonizing. On and on it went. . . .

Drip, drip, drip!

Her veins were filled to overflowing, weighting her down, down, down. . . .

She was being drawn into a long tunnel, demonic creatures grabbing at her on every side. Their grip grew tighter, tighter. . . .

"Freckle face! Freckle face!" they taunted in childish voices, long, bony fingers pointed in her direction.

Yellow roses floated by on the wind, the fragrance calling out to her—a token of purity, love, devotion. . . .

"Daddy!"

His face appeared, twisting and contorting—now the face of the most demonic of creatures imaginable.

"No! No!" she cried.

Such a father!

"You'll burn in hell for all eternity!" her Aunt Sharon jeered, face whizzing by on the wind.

"Go away! Go away!"

And yet the creatures continued to torment. Ashley could scarcely breathe as they pressed about her on every side.

Drip, drip, drip!

They were crushing her, squeezing the life, the very breath out of her.

SEVEN

Cameron Walker's breaths were shallow and fast, the cold winter air taking its toll on his lungs. Twigs and branches snapped beneath him as he ran. The thick underbrush of the forest was cutting jagged marks into his shins, but there was no time to stop and nurse them now. He was running for his very life—what was left of it, anyway.

"I want to live!"

The midmorning sun cast seemingly picturesque reflections on the heavily wooded area of East Texas, an area that—until today—would have seemed foreign to Cameron. Ribbons of green and brown faded past him as he ran—nothing but a blur, a haze.

A lover of nature, Cameron longed to stop and drink it in. What he wouldn't give for a camera, an easel. This place was calling out to him. But there wasn't time. Not now. Maybe not ever. This wasn't a day for sight-seeing. He must keep up the pace at all costs.

But, how? Exhaustion was setting in.

Tick, tick, tick. . .

His pulse pounded like a muffled drumbeat in his ears. How could he continue on without rest? Gasping for air, the young man slowed his stride, but only momentarily.

"I. . .have. . .to. . .stop!"

But he couldn't stop. Time was of the essence.

Time.

There was no time. For four long months it had been like this—ever since the day he had received the dreaded news.

HIV-positive.

His only chance for survival, temporary as it may be—a safe house deep within the woods. Sources assured him it was there. He prayed it was there. God forbid the police had already discovered the home.

God?

Hmmm. . . Well, no time for deep theological ponderings right now. More pressing matters at hand. . .

"Please be there!" Cameron cried out to the overpowering forest that surrounded him, his voice sending a reverberating, almost haunting echo.

This was his only chance, his only hope.

Hope.

What a futile word.

Cameron stopped abruptly, the vegetation in front of him suddenly growing too thick to pass through. Taking a few deep breaths, he attempted to analyze the situation. To his right, Lake Summerset. To his left, the tiny town of Cleveland. Straight ahead, the thick piney woods of East Texas. Behind him. . .

Behind him lay nothing but trouble, nothing but sure, swift death at the hands of lawmakers. He wouldn't give himself over to it, no matter what the members of Congress or medical experts said.

"Who do they think they are?" Cameron muttered, wiping sweat from his forehead with the back of his hand.

"I want to live!"

There was no turning back. Cameron must push forward. But how?

Aha, remnants of a trail. Could it be? Yes, but is it safe? His eyes shifted to and fro, analyzing the situation as quickly as he could. The terrified young man had no choice. He pushed aside brambles and weeds, watching them tear at his arms as he picked up the pace again. Blood began to flow. . .contaminated blood. No time to worry about that either. Besides, there was no one near enough to worry about—at least Cameron hoped not, for his own sake and theirs.

Tick, tick, tick. . .

His heart continued its steady cycle, churning with a force he had never before known.

Despite the cold, he began to perspire. He was overcome with heat, swallowed by it. He was aching with thirst, aching to stop and rest.

"I. . .can't. . .go. . .any. . .farther!" he mumbled, feeling everything begin to spin around him.

He was dizzy, near fainting. But he couldn't stop, wouldn't stop. . . .

"Whoa, there! Where are you going in such a hurry?" a stranger asked abruptly, stepping into view.

Cameron's heart jumped out of his chest, as he came to a quick stop.

Tick, tick, tick. . .

His hearing was muffled through the pounding of blood rushing in his ears. He could hardly make out what the old guy was saying. Who was he? Friend or foe? There was only one way to know for sure.

"I have come. . .that you might. . .have life," Cameron quoted from memory, still gasping. This week's password. Safe houses everywhere were using it.

He stared at the older man tentatively, hopefully.

"I see," the man said, suddenly grinning. "Well, why didn't you say so?"

The stranger grabbed Cameron, giving him a giant bear hug. "You must be Cameron."

Waves of pure relief swept over him. Panting and dripping with sweat, Cameron nodded. "Yes! How. . .how did you know?"

"We've been receiving coded E-mail messages for nearly three days about you. Thank God you made it. We've been very concerned." The older man stepped back, looking the younger one over. "You came from Anderson?"

"Yes," he answered, panting. "We got word we were about to be raided."

"Happened this morning," the older man confirmed. "Heard it on the news."

"Oh. . ." Cameron hardly knew what to say. "Were there any. . . I mean, did anyone? . . ."

"The only thing they found were some personal belongings and medications. No people."

Personal belongings? Cameron shuddered, remembering the box of books he had left on the floor next to the bed. His favorites were among them—Kafka's *The Metamorphosis,* Orwell, Steinbeck, and so many others.

Well, there was no time to worry about that now. At least he had made it out—and had miraculously also made it another leg of his journey.

Tick, tick, tick. . .

His heart began to slow a bit. The breaths were also coming more slowly now.

"Come on, Son. Let's go home."

Home! How good that sounded!

"You can never come home again!" the words of an angry father. *"You have disgraced our family. You are never welcome here, do you hear me? Never!"*

Cameron shook with the memory, forcing it from his mind. No one here would have to know the details of his life. It was none of their business, anyway. He stepped alongside the old man, mind full of questions. He wondered, as always, about the families who ran the safe houses. Why would they risk everything for people they didn't even know? It made no sense.

This old guy was different from the last in appearance. He looked to be between fifty-five and sixty, maybe a little older. A worn baseball cap, a T-shirt and slacks—a pretty common-looking guy. But there was an uncommon look in his eye. Something about this old man was different. Cameron was always pretty good at figuring out people and their stories—and there was certainly a story behind the eyes of this old guy.

They walked together in silence awhile before the old man finally spoke. It was really more of a whisper. . . . "HIV-positive?"

Cameron nodded, shame penetrating to the bone. So they would know after all. He still hadn't quite grown used to the idea, though he couldn't deny that his own choices, his own lifestyle must surely have brought it about.

"Well now, you're certainly not the only one here dealing with the AIDS virus."

"Oh, I'm not sick, Sir. At least not yet," Cameron assured him. "I was just diagnosed four months ago."

"Well, then. . . Looks like you're a keeper! Come on, then."

Cameron looked around him. There was no house in sight. "Where are we headed?"

"Just follow me."

There was safety in those words. Cameron stepped out in faith—either in the old man or in the powers that had guided him here, whatever they might be.

The man led the way around a chain of evergreens and past a small row of neatly planted bushes. There, tucked safely away, was a house, large and rustic. Like a chameleon it stood, blended beautifully into its scenic surroundings.

"Welcome to Havensbrook."

"Havensbrook." Cameron repeated the word.

"This is my home," the older man stated, swinging the front door open wide. "Yours too, if you'll have us."

An audience of wide eyes met him from inside the house. Men, women, children—as far as Cameron could see. He turned to face the elderly man again, listening as he jested, "As you can see, I don't live alone."

Cameron grinned. It felt good to be among people again, unproductive though they might be to society in general. He took a slow step inside, suddenly overcome by the aroma of. . .was that stew? It had been days since Cameron had eaten what anyone would call a real meal. He was suddenly very glad to be here.

"Don't be shy, Boy."

Hand after hand extended in his direction. The old man made the introductions. He started with the youngest member of the group, a young black girl about eight or nine, then moved on to the others.

"Deena Marie, sickle cell anemia. Joe Reynolds—he's seventy-two—you know what that means. Mary Lewis, multiple sclerosis. Mitsy Jansen, Alzheimer's. Jimmy Lee Thomas, leukemia. June Ann, HIV-positive."

On and on the list of names went. Handshake after handshake, hug after hug. A serene-looking elderly woman stood in the distance, not yet introduced. The older man looked at her lovingly.

"This is my wife, Abbey—the best thing that ever happened to me."

"Pleased to meet you," Cameron said, nodding her direction.

Abbey returned the nod with a warm smile. There was something really special about that smile. . . .

"And I'm Mason," the old man concluded. "Mason Wallis."

"Mason. Good to meet you—all of you," Cameron said.

"Come and sit, Son. I believe Abbey's got some food for you."

Cameron sat obligingly, watching with joy as Abbey filled a bowl with a thick, steaming ladle full of stew and placed it before him.

"Thank you," he whispered, turning to her.

Was that a wink? Yes, she had winked at him. And now a pat on the shoulder. How long had it been since his mother had treated him that way? How long? Too long to remember.

Cameron turned his attention back to the bowl of stew, unable to bear it.

Mason Wallis took a good look at his new boarder. So this was Cameron. Why, he couldn't be more than eighteen at best. To think that he had been on the run for so long. He wasn't so different from the others, really. Just someone else to love, care for. Most of his houseguests had come on a wing and a prayer, just like this one.

"We're glad to have you, Son," he said, reaching out to embrace the frightened young man. "Welcome home."

Coral Summerlin wept loudly from her double room on the maternity floor at Mercy Hospital. Just enough time had passed to let the news truly sink in. Her tears were a mixture of fear and pain—fear of the unknown and the pain of discovery that her child was something less than perfect.

"Each child is a gift of God." They had been her mother's words, heartfelt, genuine. But what kind of a giving God would place an infant in its mother's womb, only to snatch it away again? Loudly, unashamedly, Coral let the tears flow.

"Why?!?! Why?!?!"

A rustle from across the room reminded her that she was not alone.

"Could you try to keep it down over there?" the somewhat muffled voice of her roommate spoke through the drawn curtain. "I haven't slept in two days."

Frankly, Coral didn't care. There was only one thing that mattered right now—only one thing on her mind. She was finally a mother—and there was nothing, no one who could take this child away from her.

Shannon Carpenter's hand trembled as she picked up the telephone one more time. Was it too soon to try Frank again? Would he take the call? What would he say to her unbelievable news?

"Money is the thing, Shannon. It's what we live for. It's what we die for." His motto rang in her ears, causing her to hesitate.

And live for it, he did. Frank had given himself over to the pursuit of money. They were going to have the best, regardless of cost: the best home, the best cars, the best schools for the children.

"I don't fit in that world, Frank," Shannon had argued. To be

honest, she felt far more comfortable in a pair of jeans and T-shirt than designer dresses. It was frustrating, to say the least. Over the last few years, Frank had molded her into his image of what the perfect wife should be. Now, at every festive occasion, she was there on his arm, someone to impress clients with.

She had been aching for a way out of that life—hoping against hope that the tide would turn—that things would change.

Well, they had certainly changed now, hadn't they? Today's news meant that Shannon just might have to choose between her husband and a child she had never laid eyes on. One thing was for sure—regardless of her husband's response, Shannon would not—she could not—lose this child.

EIGHT

Frank Carpenter flicked the ashes from his cigarette onto the spotless, beige carpet of Congressman Paul Whitener's plush northside Houston office. Taking the toe of his expensive snakeskin boots, he ground them into the finely woven rug, leaving a small charcoal gray stain.

"Where in the Sam Hill are they?" he muttered, glancing at his Rolex.

11:00 A.M. They were supposed to be meeting at 10:45 sharp. Was he the only one with enough common courtesy to show up on time? For a moment Frank was distracted by a long, painful fit of coughing, losing the grip on the lit cigarette. These episodes had been coming more and more frequently in recent days. The tar and nicotine were taking their toll, no doubt about that.

"Nicotine is a drug with strong addictive properties." He could hear the familiar words of the television commercial in his head. *"If you're having trouble giving up cigarettes, try NickStop! NickStop stops the craving before it begins."*

He quickly tuned it out, reaching down to pick up the fallen cigarette. "I'll give 'em up," he muttered, adding, "when pigs fly."

He glanced out the window, staring at the traffic below.

"I hate this town," he muttered. He did hate it—hated everything about it. . .the noise, the confusion, the traffic. But that was tolerable for now. He was moving up—and moving on. D.C. was his ultimate goal, and he would arrive there soon enough. There he could have everything his heart desired.

"I just want a simple life, Frank." His wife's words still angered him. She would have been content to live in a duplex on the outskirts of town and play PTA mom for the next ten or fifteen years. Not him.

The door swung open suddenly, startling him.

"Frank. Sorry I'm late." Jerry Morris dropped his briefcase onto the floor next to the desk.

"Where is everyone else? I've got meetings all day. . . ," Frank complained.

"Giere isn't going to be able to make it. His kid's having his tonsils out today. And Paul. . . Well, you know Paul."

"Yes, I know Paul," he answered with some disgust.

Congressman Paul Whitener. Their fearless leader. House representative from one of Houston's more apathetic districts. Whitener commanded respect but didn't deserve it. He was always the last to show up and the first to leave. If there was dirty work to be done, he made sure someone else did it. Yes, Paul was quite the leader.

That's okay, Frank reminded himself silently. *He's my ticket out of here.*

"He's home from the Hill just so that we could meet," Jerry said. "I can't believe he missed out on the inauguration."

"I can," Frank mumbled.

"Well," Jerry added, "he's probably distracted. He's got babies to kiss, hands to shake. Always the politician."

"Hmm."

Yes, Paul was quite the politician—which is exactly why he had, in just one term in office, accomplished so much up on the Hill. Back in Houston, his prestige was building, along with his reputation for doing what it took to get what he wanted. In fact, there seemed to be little limit to what he would or wouldn't do. He had what was commonly referred to in D.C. as the magic touch.

Some magic. A disappearing act was more like it.

"Let's go ahead and start without him," Jerry said, dropping into the chair across from Frank. "Is that all right with you? I can't stay long myself."

Frank shrugged, frustrated. "Yeah. Hang on." He stretched his hand out over Paul's exquisite mahogany desk, reaching for an ashtray. There wasn't one. Frank dropped the remains of his cigarette in a nearby trash can, watching it glow with a smirk. No sooner was it extinguished than he pulled out another.

"Got a light?" he asked Jerry. "I'm out of matches."

"The whole county's out of matches since you picked up the habit," Jerry said smugly.

"Very funny."

"Kidding," Jerry said, reaching into his pocket, pulling out a small, gold lighter. "You smoke too much, though," he said plainly, tossing the lighter in Frank's direction. "Don't you ever read the warnings on those things?" he mumbled.

Frank shrugged as he caught the lighter. Quickly he lit the cigarette, taking a long, slow drag. "Ah. . . Now that's better," he said, leaning back in the chair. Jerry rolled his eyes.

"What's the latest from the Hill?" Frank asked, ready to get down to business.

"Well, Tinsdale's feeling the pressure to come on board," Jerry said. "I know you're concerned. I am, too. But we have to give her some time."

"Time? Who has time? I don't have time. Do you have time?" Frank's words were curt.

"You worry too much, Frank," Jerry argued. "You always have. I think we're in pretty good shape. I'm content with the way things are progressing. Besides, what can she do? We're talking about the law of the land here. . .one that her predecessor signed."

"Don't I know it." Here Frank hesitated. It was a law that he had helped draft. A law that he had struggled with at its core. It was a law that he had watched waffle through Congress, finally hitting the president's desk at the end of his four-year term. It was a law that had been signed immediately by then-President Alfred Klingerman.

Frank had struggled with mixed feelings in the beginning, but they had passed quickly. The chance to work with a famous congressman like Whitener had temporarily overshadowed any opposition he might have had. He was easily persuaded, once the situation presented itself in full array. This was about opportunity, pure and simple. So what if his conscience was a little seared? He managed, as always, to push it down.

Over the last few months, Frank had developed a new outlook on life—or perhaps a new outlook on death would be a better way to put it. It had been necessary to mull through his emotions on the matter, since "the matter" seemed to consume his days and nights. He had concluded, with no reservations, that it all boiled down to a simple matter of practicality. "Survival of the fittest"—a concept going all the way back to seventh-grade science.

Besides, he was now convinced, from every conceivable angle, and every legal angle, that they had done the right thing. But his conviction certainly wasn't an indication that everyone felt that way. . . .

"Has there been any more trouble?" he asked hesitantly.

There was always trouble. Just getting the Duty to Die bill through Congress had been a nightmare. Right to Lifers at every turn, rearing their ugly heads, caused endless delays. Frank saw them only as obstacles to his political aspirations, nothing more.

But trouble with the Pro-Lifers had always been a thorn in his flesh, especially these days—since the law had passed.

"Nothing major," Jerry stated. "We're still trying to work out the details on the pending bill."

"Ah, yes. There was another bill yet to come. The Suicide Kit. This would offer a how-to suicide manual and form of request for lethal drugs for any American citizen requesting it. Sensible. . .at least to many. These folks were often in severe pain, struggling with diseases that didn't carry the title "terminal." Many were fighting emotional battles—the loss of a loved one, a struggle with hopelessness.

They needed someone to reach out to.

These were people who were going to attempt suicide anyway. Why not give them a clean, antiseptic way to do it? Frank almost saw himself as a benefactor to these people—someone who would go down in the history books as one who had cared about those no one else had cared for. Of course, the income from the Suicide Kit would put a little extra money into the government health care program, but who could argue with that?

"The courts will continue to back us up," Jerry continued. "All over the country they're striking down state laws that seek to ban assisted suicide. Their rulings have been crystal clear—sending out a pretty strong message."

"I think it's amazing—what's happened in the courts," Frank said.

More than amazing. Even before the new law had taken effect, the courts had already begun to look at two classes: those that the state had a higher calling to protect—the young, those who were stronger or only temporarily ill—and those in which the state's interest was "less essential"—the terminally ill, etc.

It was only the "etc." that concerned Frank.

"Not to worry, my friend," Jerry said with a smile. "We've got friends in high places. That's all that matters now."

They did, indeed.

"Anything else?" Frank asked tentatively.

"Yes," Jerry said anxiously. "We've got to get a grip on the underground movement. So far, we're not doing very well in containing them."

Frank sighed. The intervention groups were big problems and needed to be stopped. They were getting in the way.

"That's why I thought we should meet today," Jerry explained, looking toward the door.

Where was Paul? He should have been here by now.

Jerry continued, oblivious to Frank's frustration. "There's got to be something more we can do."

"There's always more," Frank muttered.

"The good news is," Jerry said, "elimination units are popping up right and left. Before you know it, every hospital across the country will have one."

"Crossings Units?" Frank asked with a nod.

"They go by different names. Most are calling themselves 'the Bridge,' or 'the Crossing,' or something to that effect."

"Wording is important," Frank agreed, lighting another cigarette.

"NickStop. . .stops the craving before it begins."

"What did you say?" he stammered.

"I said, yes. It's the determining factor," Jerry responded, looking at him quizzically. "Are you okay?"

"Great. Great. Uh, what's your take on how the public is reacting to all of this?" Frank asked, looking Jerry in the eye. "Are we winning them over?" He really wanted to know. The public had to be behind them, or this whole thing was useless.

Jerry paused. "For the most part. Any change, especially something this big, is bound to take awhile. But we've started educating the very youngest ones already. There are programs already in place, beginning in the elementary school classroom. By the time our kids are grown, we won't even be having discussions like this."

The door swung open quickly, giving both men a start. Paul Whitener had arrived.

"I've asked you not to smoke in my office, Frank," he said abruptly. "It's against the law. You know that."

The law. Now there was something Paul would know about.

"Glad you could join us," Frank said, somewhat sarcastically, dropping more ashes onto the carpet the moment Paul's back was turned.

"Did I miss much?" Paul dropped into the plush seat behind his mahogany desk.

"We haven't gotten very far," Frank responded, agitated at Paul's obvious apathy.

"Well now. . . What's so important that I had to give up my racquetball game this afternoon, gentlemen?" Paul asked.

"Racquetball?" Frank mumbled.

"I'm a busy guy," Paul said with a grin. "What can I say?"

Frank pulled the cigarette out of his mouth long enough to say what he felt needed to be said, "It's the intervention groups, Paul. Jerry seems to think we're not doing enough. . . ."

"I think we'd better come up with some plan for tracking them down and dealing with them," Jerry added, shrugging.

"Don't we have the appropriate people in place already?" Frank argued. "I've got my people working night and day on a tracking system, similar to the one that's already in place in the criminal justice system. We're going to begin planting microchips under the skin the moment each patient enters the elimination unit."

"It's not enough," Jerry said quickly. "We're not getting the job done during what I call the 'shock' period—the time between when they're diagnosed and when they are supposed to enter the unit. We're losing them right and left during those crucial weeks."

"We've been able to track down a few and bring them back," Frank added, pressing the cigarette into extinction in the crystal ashtray.

"But our percentages are low," Jerry threw in. "We've got to start a public awareness campaign, make it beneficial for the people out there to start turning some of these folks in. And we've got to pursue some of these intervention groups more rapidly—stop them at their core."

"Oh, I agree," Paul said, picking up the telephone. With the push of a button he had his secretary on the line. "Linda, make a call to Jerome Patterson," he spoke brusquely into the receiver. "Tell him that I'd like to meet with him as soon as possible."

"Who's Jerome Patterson?" Frank whispered in Jerry's direction.

"Got me."

"He's a private investigator," Paul said, hanging up the phone. "He's done some work for me in the past."

"We're calling in someone from the outside?" Frank asked incredulously. "I thought we all agreed it would be better to keep things tight at the top."

"This can be done carefully," Paul said, standing. "Besides, he's one of my guys. Now, if you fellas don't mind, I've got an, uh, appointment with a cute little blond. You wouldn't want to make me late, would you?"

Jerry and Frank stared at each other in disbelief. "You're leaving?"

"Sure," Paul said, opening the office door and gesturing for the men to exit. "We all are."

Another long fit of coughing caught Frank by surprise as he stood to his feet. As if on cue, Paul reached across his desk, picking up the half-empty pack of cigarettes Frank had left lying there. He tossed the pack in Frank's direction, his words laced with sarcasm. "Have another cigarette, Frank."

Frank's insides burned. Congressman or no congressman, this guy was getting no respect from him.

The others were hardly out the door before Frank's mobile phone rang. Frustrated, he struggled to get it out of his briefcase before he lost the call altogether.

"Hello. . . Hello!"

Shannon Carpenter's heart raced as she heard her husband's familiar voice. He sounded angry. Maybe this wasn't a good time.

"Who is this?" Frank demanded from the other end of the line.

"It's me, Honey," she said finally.

"Don't scare me like that, Shannon. It's not funny."

"I'm not trying to be funny, Frank. I just. . .need to talk to you."

"This isn't a good time right now. Can I call you when I get back to the office?"

"No, Frank. This can't wait."

"What is so all-fired important? I am in the middle of something."

Shannon braced herself, unsure of how he would take the news. "I. . .I just took a pregnancy test."

"You what?"

She had expected him to be surprised, shocked. Shannon should have told him of her suspicions long before now. She knew that now. But she had just kept hoping, praying. . . .

"You heard me," she said, her voice quavering. "I took a pregnancy test." She paused, unable to continue.

"Sometime today, Shannon." His words were curt, short.

Her heart was really racing now. She summoned up the courage to speak the dreaded words, praying that she could live with his response. "It was positive."

Dead silence.

"Well," he spoke finally, forcefully. "What are you going to do about it?"

"Do about it? What do you mean?"

"You can't be pregnant, Shannon," he answered angrily. "You, of all people, should know that. There's a lot more at stake here than you know. You've got to get rid of it."

Tears worked their way out of her eyes. So this was how it was going to be. No sympathy. No responsibility. A simple solution to a bothersome problem—a problem that stood in the way of his precious job.

"No, Frank. It's not that easy. I don't think I can. . . ."

"Of course you can," he answered, agitated. "Women have abortions every day. Besides, what other choice do you have?"

Choices?

That was a question Shannon simply had no answer for. Of course, he was right. As soon as her pregnancy was discovered, she would be forced to undergo an abortion, anyway—followed by a mandatory sterilization. Two children per family. No exceptions. That was the law. But it wasn't right. Someone should say something. Someone should *do* something.

"Do something!"

"I just thought. . ."

"Thought what? We're dealing with a federal law here, Shannon—a law resulting from a bill that I helped draft."

"We can go away," she stammered. "We could move."

"Move?"

"You have always wanted to get away—get out of here," she argued.

"Not like this. Besides, where would we go?"

"I was thinking about that job offer you had a couple of years ago in London. It sounded really good. And we wouldn't have to worry about the children there."

"That's not going to happen, Shannon," he said firmly, angrily. "You're going to do the right thing."

"The right thing?" she asked, feeling anger well up inside her.

"Yes, the right thing," he responded. "You know what I mean."

"But. . ."

"No buts. Just let me take care of everything," Frank said. "And whatever you do, don't tell anyone. You can't trust anyone."

"But. . ."

"Just stay put. I'm on my way home."

Shannon dropped onto the plush sofa, trembling uncontrollably. She was too tired to debate the issue any further. Her mind argued that she must go through with the abortion. Her heart convinced her otherwise. . . .

Charlotte Tinsdale was shaking all over as the ceremony came to a close. She had never been so excited—or so nervous—in all of her forty-seven years. Reaching down, she clutched the hands of her two sons, Matthew and Jonathan.

"You did great, Mom!" eleven-year-old Jonathan said, reaching up to hug her.

"That's Madame President to you, Kid!" she said jokingly.

"Not bad—for a woman," fourteen-year-old Matthew chimed.

Charlotte held them both tightly, feeling the lump in her throat. There was only one thing that could have made this moment really perfect—if her husband, Pete, had lived to see it.

She turned to face the crowd once again, their applause almost deafening.

NINE

Drip, drip, drip!

No! No! Stop it! The sound was unbearable to Ashley's ears. *I want to live!* Just as the noise reached a painful high—a blast of light!

Light?

A glaring, blinding shaft of light was penetrating her being, searing to the very core of her being. Was it possible? She was alive!

Or was she? Ashley still felt the pain. It was as if a thousand-pound weight sat on her chest, crushing the very life out of her.

Tick, tick, tick. . .

Dear God, no! she tried to scream. She gasped for breath, still tasting the toxins in her saliva. Was she alive? If so, where was she? Still in the hospital room, perhaps? Ashley tried to force her eyes to focus on the room around her. . .a wall, painted in a haze of violet—a window with heavy curtains—a watercolor painting of a picturesque mountain setting. The colors ran together in a swirling mass.

No. This was a different place. Even through the confusion of the moment, Ashley could tell that. She blinked rapidly, the light above nearly blinding her.

Tick, tick, tick. . .

She heard it again. Following the sound with her eyes,

Ashley found herself looking into the face of a small bedroom clock. 11:36.

Bedroom? Yes, she did appear to be lying in a bed, but whose? And how?

Carefully, she tried to speak. To her amazement, the words tumbled out, almost easily. "Where. . .where am I?"

The now-familiar face of the young doctor peered down at her. Their eyes met in a fixed stare. Instinctively, she began to tremble.

No! It was him. She had to get out of here. . .get away. But how?

"I'm not going to hurt you, Ashley," he said quietly, almost gently. "I brought you here. You're safe with me."

He was calling her by name. Did he know her? Ashley's mind raced, trying to piece together the events that had just happened. Did she know this man? Could she really trust him?

The shaking subsided a little. Ashley felt a hand grip hers, squeezing tightly. "He saved your life, Honey," a familiar voice spoke from the other side.

"Mama?!?!" She turned to look her beautiful mother in the eye. Suddenly the pain didn't matter anymore. The joy of her discovery was worth it all. "Where am I?" she asked, trying to sit up. "How did I get here?"

"Just lie still, Honey," her mother said, patting her on the shoulder. "You've been through quite an ordeal, and you need your rest."

Ashley couldn't seem to sit up, anyway. She was far too weak, too sick. And the pain in her chest was still overwhelming. "I. . .I can't breathe," she gasped.

The doctor pulled out an oxygen mask, placing it over her mouth and nose. "Take deep breaths if you can, Ashley. We're trying to counteract the poison. It's taken its toll on your lungs. But you have to help us."

Poison? Ah, yes. The poison—the reason she was in Mercy Hospital in the first place.

Cancer. Incurable.

Ashley's mind began to race. She was supposed to be dead. People in her place didn't get second chances. No one was above the law. She looked up at her mother. There was so much she wanted to ask her, tell her. But she couldn't speak now. The pain was far too intense.

Ashley began to breathe deeply, attempting to relax. The pain in her chest was beginning to ease somewhat. After what seemed like an eternity, she was finally able to breathe evenly— without the searing pain. The oxygen mask was removed.

"I guess I. . .I owe you an apology," she mumbled, looking up at the young doctor with new eyes, new-found respect and gratitude.

"What do you mean?"

He had saved her life. He wasn't her enemy after all. She could hardly wait to thank him, to ask question after question. There must be some reason why her life was spared.

"You, you saved me! I thought you were. . ."

"The enemy?" he asked, laughing. "That's what you were supposed to think. I've got to come across that way. It's my cover."

Ashley tried once again to sit up. It took every ounce of energy. Her mother propped up pillows behind her, and she was almost able to get comfortable.

"Okay," she said finally, taking slow, deep breaths. "Tell me everything. Where am I? How did I get here? Do I have to go back to the hospital? Are we in trouble?"

"Whoa! Slow down, Girl," the young doctor said, smiling. "Don't make me pull out that oxygen mask again!"

Ashley forced a smile. Apparently he was trying to be funny. Her eyes searched out her mother. Surely she would know.

"We asked for an intervention," Angela Cooper said defiantly, "and we got one."

"Intervention?" Ashley asked her mother.

"An intervention is. . ."

"I know what the word means," she said. "I just need to know how it applies to me."

"I'm trying to explain," Aaron answered.

Ashley focused her attention on the young man once again. No longer a stranger to be feared, she now read the trust in his eyes.

"Several of us in the medical community are completely and unequivocally opposed to the new law," the young doctor explained. "It's a slap in the face to those of us who feel that we're supposed to be saving lives, not taking them. So we created this. . . organization."

"Organization?"

"I guess you could call it a network. There are hundreds, no, really thousands of us around the country who refuse to submit to the new law. It's unconscionable to us. So we perform these, these. . .interventions. We're a pretty well-organized group."

"Underground?" Ashley asked, her heart beginning to race once again. "Won't they catch you?" She didn't want to go back. She would never go back!

"It's a risk worth taking, especially in cases like yours."

"Cases like mine?"

"You were diagnosed with a rare form of cancer, is that right?"

Ashley nodded. "Yes." It had come as a complete shock.

"They told you there was no cure, I'm sure. . . ."

Prognosis: death.

Of course there was no cure. That's why she was put on the terminal list. That's what she was doing in Crossings in the first place. Surely he understood that. He might have saved her life—but only temporarily. The cancer was going to kill her soon anyway.

"Ashley, there's something you need to know."

Not more bad news.

"Tell me. I can take it," she said, swallowing hard. She was strong. Or was she? Right now Ashley was just confused and very, very weak.

"You're not terminal, Ashley," Angela said quickly, firmly. "At least. . .we don't think so."

Ashley turned to look her mother in the eye. There were

tears streaming down her face. Obviously her mother was in denial. "Mama, you know I am. You saw the doctor's reports."

"No, Ashley. There are treatments available."

"What?"

"I guess they didn't tell you that part, did they?" Aaron asked, a hint of a smile crossing his lips. "I'm planning on getting my hands on your records, but if what your mother has told me is true, you've got a fighting chance. And I'd like to be the one to give it to you."

"This isn't funny."

"No. It's not funny," Aaron said, feeling the tension of the moment. "It's serious. Deadly serious. They're taking patients who have a high potential for cure and killing them off."

"But why?"

It was a logical question—and one that he had the answer to. "Several reasons, I guess. It all started with managed health care, if you ask me. If just seemed like people who needed certain treatment simply weren't getting it because it wasn't, I don't know, cost efficient, I guess you'd say."

"It didn't start out that way," Ashley's mother, Angela, threw in. "Remember, Honey—I worked in billing at a managed health-care facility years ago."

Aaron watched as she nodded. For the first time he was able to take a good long look at the young woman he had rescued. She was petite, and pretty—very pretty.

"What does that have to do with me?" she asked.

"Even the best of intentions can go astray if the wrong people get involved," Aaron continued. "Suddenly it was all about money —who could get it and who would give it. . . . The elderly and terminally ill were the first affected. Later it was everyone who required any type of surgery or major medical treatment. And then came government health care. . . ."

"What do you mean?" Ashley asked, looking puzzled.

Aaron knew all too well. It was just about the time he had lost his parents—the worse possible time in his life.

"The story began to change pretty drastically after that," he said, trying to push the memory from his mind. "Funny thing was, it was almost like people didn't see what was happening right under their noses. If they did, they were the most apathetic bunch I've ever seen. For the sake of the almighty dollar, good, honest working people—taxpayers, no less—were tossed by the wayside, left to die or pray for a miracle."

"Some miracle," Angela muttered. "Duty to Die."

"It was their only answer, really," Aaron said. "But it didn't start out that way. The government, along with the medical community—and here's where I come in—created a sort of yardstick to measure human worth. They started weighing what they called ordinary care against extraordinary care. All this making sense?"

Ashley nodded slowly.

He continued. "Anyone who required extraordinary care would be euthanized, plain and simple. When I first heard about it, I was just starting med school. It made me sick. I can't tell you how it affected me."

It was affecting him even now.

"At that time," he said, "the infants and the indigent were just beginning to be targeted. Then, of course, came 'Duty to Die.' "

"Their answer. . ."

"It hasn't been an answer—not even close—but they're banking on it, just the same. The government can't seem to keep up with rising costs of treatments and medications for those with simple illnesses—and then there's the issue of organ donation and medical research. Why spend money saving a life when you can use the body parts for someone who has the resources to pay big money under the table?"

Ashley voice trembled as she spoke. "They could have cured me, and they decided to kill me instead?"

Aaron nodded emphatically. "That's right. You were about to become more valuable to them dead than alive. It happens every day. You've heard of the slippery slope, haven't you?"

Ashley shook her head. Their eyes met, but for a moment.

Ashley turned away nervously. "Well, yes, but—I mean, I'm sorry —but I never really got involved in that debate. It was just too. . ."

"Touchy?"

"Yeah."

"Touchier now than ever, don't you agree? Wasn't it inevitable that the right to die would eventually become the duty to die?" Aaron asked, looking her in the eye. "What started out as an exception would have to become the rule—that's always the way things go."

Ashley sat in stony silence.

"A brave few voiced their concerns from the very beginning," Aaron said.

He had been among them—starting in 1973 with the momentous court decision that had flipped America's moral system up on its ear.

"You were one of them?" Ashley asked.

He nodded without hesitation. "Yes, even as a child, I think I recognized the problem. . . . It always seemed obvious, at least to me, that a country willing to sacrifice its young would eventually begin to devalue all forms of life. I mean, it was just a matter of time before other lives would be required for sacrifice."

"Sacrifice?"

"Yes. But those who spoke up were usually stifled by the media. Or, worse yet, they were made to look like idiots."

"Who makes the decisions—about who will live and who will die?" Ashley demanded, her face flushed.

"Anyone and everyone," Aaron answered. "We're all just pawns in a high-stakes chess game. The chief players are. . .well, to be honest—they're all around us. You might be surprised at just how many of our representatives in Congress are actually bought out by powerful attorneys and lobbying groups."

A lone tear slipped down Ashley's cheek.

"You need your rest, Baby," Angela said, reaching out to take her hand.

"No. I need to know. . .about the treatment. What are you

talking about, exactly? Can I take it now?"

"There is a relatively new drug, SU5368, that's been highly effective against the type of cancer you're fighting. And there are others still in the laboratory, not even tried on humans. Used in combination with aloe vera, enzymes, and even common herbs, some of them are projected to be extremely potent in treating most types of cancer, even in its later stages. But it's not approved yet."

"Why not?" she demanded, suddenly feeling nauseated.

"I told you. . . ."

"Yes. You told me. But if there's a treatment, I want it!"

"And I'm going to make sure that you get it," Aaron said, smiling. "Just trust me."

Should she trust him? That was a tough question. How could she when everyone else had already let her down?

Aaron watched as she relaxed against the pillows. Ashley looked up into his eyes one last time.

He took her hand, giving it a squeeze.

"It's going to be okay," he said. "I promise."

She nodded, drifting off to sleep almost immediately. Aaron stared long and hard at her. What a long morning this had been—a nerve-wracking, exhausting morning. And yet, it was at times like this, he had to remind himself that it was worth it all—worth risking his medical license, even worth risking his very life.

There was a sparkle in this young woman's eyes just moments ago—a look of hope that had not been there before. He had been responsible for that, at least to some extent. It felt good, mighty good.

And now, the moment of truth. He had promised her a cure. It was time to mix some action with his faith.

Hannah Gilbert took a few extra moments to pick some flowers for her sister before going back inside. She paused at the walkway, glancing up at the old, wood-framed house, content in the fact that God was in His heaven, and all was right with the world. In spite of the law. In spite of Molly's attitude. In spite of everything.

It had been quite a morning. Her trip to the market had been pleasant and profitable. She had met friends along the way and had been given plenty of opportunity to spread a little sunshine around. The bigger challenge awaited her inside the door.

Taking a deep breath, she stepped inside.

"Sister?" she called out. "Sister? I'm home!"

TEN

Shannon Carpenter hit the brake, tires squealing mercilessly. The Lexus came grinding to a halt, barely missing the beat-up truck in front of it.

"Hold on!" she hollered back to the kids. It had been a narrow miss, caused by her own carelessness.

The driver of the truck hit his horn, waving his arm out of the open window and shouting, "Who gave you a license, Lady? You think just because you drive a car like that, you own the road?"

Shannon's heart sank, and fear overwhelmed her. It was dangerous to get drivers riled up in the city. Who knew what might happen? Shannon waited breathlessly, hoping that he would move on without incident. Thankfully, he did. She pulled out into the other lane and continued on her way, picking up speed, lost in thought.

"Mommy!" Veronica's high-pitched squeal riveted her.

"Are you okay?" Shannon asked, hitting the brakes.

"You're scaring me, Mom!" the six year old said from the back seat. "Why do you have to drive so fast?"

"Can't you drive any faster?"

Why the words hit her now, she wasn't sure, but they sent her reeling.

"Do something!"

But nothing could be done. It was too late, too. . .

77

From the back seat, Zachary was now crying loudly. "Mommy! Mommy!"

"Zachary, Honey. . ." Shannon heard her own words but couldn't seem to separate them from that night three years ago. . . .

"Where were you?!"

"Mommy, slow down," Veronica spoke, almost angrily.

"I'm sorry, Honey," Shannon said, snapping. "How's Gilligan?"

She heard the yip and knew the puppy was fine.

"He's scared, Mom," Veronica said. "I am, too. I want to go home!"

"I'm so scared!"

Words from the past, again.

"Where are we going?" Veronica interrupted her thoughts.

"I. . .I don't know." Where was she going, anyway? Shannon wasn't sure. There was only one thing she did know for sure—she was not going to keep the appointment with the abortionist today like Frank had instructed.

She couldn't. She wouldn't.

Staring at her image in the rearview mirror, Shannon asked herself the important question: *Do you have the courage?* . . . The face in the mirror stared back. The question remained unanswered.

Aaron Landers stared at his own face in the mirror, trying to get alone with his thoughts. There were so many unanswered questions in his mind. What could he do to help Ashley? Was he really capable of helping anyone at all?

No, he determined, staring intently at his own reflection. He wasn't capable. But he certainly knew someone Who was.

The White House.

It was a frightfully huge place, and about as homey as a mausoleum. For the last couple of days, Charlotte had wandered through the rooms that were now hers—trying to drink it all in. Could this really be happening, or was it all just a dream?

"You okay, Mom?" Her fourteen-year-old son popped out from behind the door, startling her.

"Matt, you scared me!" Everything here scared her, but she didn't add that.

"Sorry."

"Yeah, I'm okay," she answered hesitantly. "I've just got a lot on my mind."

"Thinking about Dad?"

She was, indeed. But how did he always seem to know? Matt was so much like his father, it was scary at times.

"I wish he were here," Charlotte said, placing her arm around Matt's shoulder. "He would have loved this."

Matt nodded. "He always said we would get to the White House someday!"

"I know," she whispered. "But I always thought it would be him. . . ."

"When you're elected," Charlotte said with a giggle, "we'll steal the towels from the White House bathroom."

"Why?" her husband, Pete, argued. "They'll be our towels, won't they?"

"When you live in the White House," Charlotte said, "nothing is yours!"

That much was true, as she was quickly learning. But getting to the White House had always been their dream.

"I'll tell the chef what to prepare for dinner," Charlotte said, pulling him close, "and we'll ask for room service."

"Since when does the president of the United States have time for room service?" Pete argued.

She had only shrugged her response. Their future loomed before them, like a hope—a dream. Now, without him, it was feeling a little more like a nightmare. Overwhelmed, she pulled her son into her arms.

"You okay?" he asked, sounding a little muffled.

"Yeah, why?"

"Well," he said, "I'm having a little trouble breathing here."

"Oh," she said, loosening her grip. "Sorry!"

They had a good laugh together. Charlotte looked into Matt's face, seeing Pete all over again. Her boys were. . .boys were. . .

"Where's Jonathan?" she asked abruptly.

"In the pool."

"It's January!"

"It's heated, remember?"

"Oh, yeah."

"It's gonna be okay, Mom," he said, laughing. "Everything's gonna be okay."

"I hope you're right."

They were all the words she could muster.

There were no words to express how Coral Summerlin was feeling. She reached inside the incubator to run her finger across Baby Jamie's cheek. It was soft and pink—just as a baby's skin should be. Everything about him was as it should be.

Except the obvious.

"Are you sure I can't pick him up?" she asked the charge nurse. Coral gave it her best face, knowing the answer was inevitable.

"I'm sorry, Mrs. Summerlin, but you know better than that."

She did, indeed. How often had she been told? How many times had she pleaded, hoped?

"It doesn't make any sense," Coral muttered for the umpteenth time. Her arms hung limply at her side, a sign of utter defeat.

"They don't want you to bond," the nurse explained for probably the tenth or eleventh time. "Just makes things harder."

Harder? How could anything be harder than it already was? This whole thing had passed the point of absurdity long ago.

"Look, Honey, I don't make the rules. I just enforce them."

Coral nodded, defeated. For the better part of the last day and a half at Mercy Hospital, she had kept a vigil here at her son's side in the nursery of Crossings Unit. Rocking chairs framed this large, uninviting room that housed those born to die. Other mothers sat nearby, unable to hold or nurse their infants. The law wouldn't allow it. Their eyes often met hers in wide-eyed, fearful glances. And then, just as quickly, they would turn their gazes back to their own children.

Full of milk, and readier than ever to hold Baby Jamie, Coral had to reconcile herself to a finger run across his cheek when no one was looking. It had almost been enough to pacify her. Until today. Today she was being released, free to go home—without him.

"Okay, the green wallpaper, then."

"And when he's two or three," Jacob said, "we'll get him one of those beds shaped like a little car."

"You mean, when she's two or three," Coral had argued.

But she was a he. Jacob had been right all along. This little "he" needed to be in his nursery at home. It had been prepared just for him, and now it was sitting empty—awaiting his arrival. How could that be right?

How could she leave him? She couldn't! How could any mother be asked to leave her own flesh and blood behind?

"Are you sure I can't? . . ." she asked.

The nurse shook her head, growing angry. "You're just making my job harder. You don't want to get me fired, do you?"

Coral wasn't thinking about the nurse right now. All she could think about was that beautiful infant lying in front of her, untouched, unloved. She was his mother. She deserved, at the very least, a touch.

Cameron sat quietly in the tiny cubicle of a room he had been given at Havensbrook, running his fingers across the picture in his hand. His mother's face smiled back at him, a photograph worn with time and travel. How he longed for her touch.

"Just a touch, Mom! Just one hug! That's all I'm asking for."

Cameron's mind was drifting, thinking back to the look on his parents' faces the day he had given them the news, the terrible, tragic news that would change his life—and theirs—forever. . . .

He could hardly bear to think of it now. Everything he had hoped for—college, career in art—everything was over.

Defeated by the thought, his hand went limp. The picture fell to the ground.

Dr. Blaine Bishop reached down to the linoleum floor, picking up the ink pen that had slipped from his coat pocket. He stared intently at it.

"Mercy Hospital," it read.

"Some mercy," Blaine mumbled, shoving it into his pocket.

He picked up the chart for a new patient, a baby boy born with Down's syndrome. This one still had a few weeks before he met up with the inevitable. Blaine sighed deeply, looking over the infant's chart.

"Never stood a chance," he mumbled, flipping through it. "He'll never make it out of here alive."

"Murderer!"

The word slapped him clean across the face, hard and fast.

"Murderer!"

Blaine shoved the chart closed, turning quickly toward the door.

"I am not taking this anymore! I've got to get out of here!" the words were meant as much for his own ears as those nearby.

"Everything okay, Doctor?" Nurse Gina Evans asked, her face an obvious mixture of confusion and doubt.

"If anyone wants me," Blaine answered curtly, "I'll be at home!"

"I do believe I have finally found the solution to my dilemma," Molly Gilbert said, turning from the television set. "If you care to hear it."

"What is that, Sister?" Hannah asked, putting her magazine down. Molly had hardly spoken a word for the last couple of days.

Hannah would give her the undivided attention she desired.

"I'm going to end my own life—before they get to me."

"I beg your pardon?" Hannah heard the words but hardly knew what to think of them. Surely Molly was kidding. "You can't be serious!"

"I'm as serious as a heart attack," Molly said. "Never spoke a more serious word in my life. Even ordered a book on the subject."

"Ordered a book?" Hannah asked, amazed. "How? When?"

"Over the Internet," Molly said smugly. "Just minutes ago, when you were out gallivanting about with that ridiculous purple hat on again. You don't think you're the only one who knows how to travel the Information Superhighway, do you?"

Hannah didn't know how to respond. Molly had rarely touched the computer in the two years they had owned it. As far as she knew, Molly didn't even know how to turn the contraption on. How in the world did she? . . . Well, at any rate, this was a conversation that needed pursuing.

"Tell me about the book, Mol," Hannah said firmly.

Molly shrugged. "Not much to tell. It's just a how-to kind of a book. . . ."

"How-to? How to what?" She knew the answer but felt compelled to ask anyway. These books were gaining popularity, especially among the elderly.

"*Ten Steps to a Peaceful Passage.* That's what it's called," Molly answered. "I figure if I've got to go, it's going to be on my terms. You know. . .my own way, in my own time."

"When you go," Hannah said, teeth clenched, "it's going to be God's way, in God's time! That's not your decision to make, Molly Gilbert." She was suddenly shaking with anger. Molly had no right to do this. No right!

Her older sister simply shrugged. "I'm just being practical, that's all."

"Not a very practical idea to my way of thinking," Hannah argued, trying to push the anger down to a workable level. "It's downright selfish! How dare you suggest such a thing!"

"It's nobody's business but my own," Molly argued.

"I beg to differ! I'm not ready to spend the rest of my days without you," Hannah stammered. "And what about everyone else?"

"Who?"

"The folks up at the church, just to name a few. And your nieces and nephews. . . They all need you, all love you."

"Fiddlesticks," Molly mumbled. "Ain't nobody cares a lick about me—or you either, for that matter. I bought this book for the both of us, don't you know. . . ."

Hannah's blood began to boil. "Well, you can count me out, Molly Gilbert!" she all but shouted. "I've got a lot of living left to do!"

"It's not as bad as you think," Molly grumbled. "Not even complicated. . . A handful of pills to swallow, maybe even a simple injection. . ."

"You hate needles," Hannah reminded her. "You always have."

Molly shrugged. "I never said I was going to take that route. It was just a comment. I'm weighing all of my options, that's all."

"Well, there's one option you've apparently left out."

"What's that?"

"Hope," Hannah said firmly.

"Hope?"

"Yes, hope! You've given up all hope, Molly Gilbert. Why, I'm downright ashamed of you!"

"Just wait 'til you're sixty-eight," Molly argued. "Then you'll understand the meaning of hopeless."

"You're only sixty-seven."

"Whatever. You are deliberately missing my point."

"Oh, you've made your point—loud and clear," Hannah said, glaring. "But one thing is for doggone sure. The minute that book arrives, it's going straight in the trash can."

"Oh, no it's not!" Molly argued. "I paid $29.95 for that book, and I'm going to read it—if it's the last thing I do!"

"It just might be," Hannah mumbled.

"Besides," Molly continued, obliviously. "It would be a waste of good money to buy a book and not read it."

"This whole conversation is a waste of good time and sense, if you ask me!" Hannah answered. She turned from the room, tears in her eyes. There had to be something she could do to snap her sister out of this.

ELEVEN

So what are we doing here, Madame President? What's the plan?"

Charlotte stared at her reflection in the mirror, pondering the older woman's question. Did she have a plan? She was the president of the United States. She was supposed to have all of the answers. Every child in America was counting on her to have the answers. Every mother. Every father. And yet she wasn't sure how to respond to even the simplest of things.

"I guess," she said slowly. "I guess I should. . ."

"This ain't no economic summit, Honey," the woman continued. "I'm just here to touch up your hair. You tell me how much to cut, and I'll cut."

Madge had come highly recommended, had easily gained the appropriate clearance, but Charlotte still wasn't sure about her qualifications. A bit offbeat, the quirky woman wore her own frizzy hair in a shocking mane of red-orange, twisted back with lime green rubber bands, tiny plastic frogs perched on top. Could she really be trusted to trim the hair of the president of the United States of America?

"You tell me not to cut, I won't cut," Madge continued, pulling the scissors away.

"No," Charlotte said firmly. "It's got to come off—at least in part. My advisors tell me that I'm too feminine. They want me to have more of a business look."

She tended to disagree, but. . .

"Nothing wrong with being too feminine," Madge said, taking a step back. "Don't let them turn you into a man, Hon. If I cut too much, you'll look just like every other president before you."

"Very funny."

"Someone's gotta have a sense of humor," the hairdresser said with a smirk. "No one around this place ever seems to crack a smile."

"You've been here before?" Charlotte looked at her curiously.

"Sure. I've been cuttin' hair here for as long as I can remember," Madge said. "Presidents' wives, children. . ."

"No presidents?"

"Nah. They always had their own personal barbers. You're my first president."

"That's quite an honor."

"Thanks. So what's it gonna be?" Madge asked again. "And don't give me that stuff about what they want. Tell me what you want."

What she wanted? Wow. It had been a long time since anyone had cared about what she wanted.

"To be honest," Charlotte said, "I really like the length in back. The top could stand to be trimmed a little. And you know what I'd like, honestly?"

"What, Hon?"

"I'd like some highlights," Charlotte said, coming to life. "Just a few to soften up the area around my face. I don't want to come across looking too harsh on camera."

"Now you're talking," Madge said, beginning to clip away. "Now you're talking." The older woman hummed an unfamiliar tune as she worked, a pleasant sound.

"What's that?" Charlotte asked. "I don't think I know it."

"Oh. Just an old hymn," Madge said, pulling up a lock of hair to trim it. " 'It Is Well with My Soul.' "

"I've never heard of it." It did have a soothing sound.

Madge sang softly as she cut. . . .

" 'When peace like a river attendeth my way, when sorrows like sea billows roll; Whatever my lot, Thou has taught me to say, It is well, it is well with my soul.' "

It was beautiful. But there was something more. There seemed to be a special message in the song, something meant just for her. Charlotte needed that kind of peace, especially with the chaos of her current situation.

"You a Christian, Honey?" Madge asked the question abruptly, startling her.

Charlotte answered the only way she knew how. "I was raised in church. I guess you could say I'm a Christian."

"Being raised in a church don't make you a Christian any more than living in a garage makes you a car."

Well, that was logic. Certainly something to think about.

Charlotte sat silently for awhile, listening to the swishing of the scissors against her hair. It, combined with the gentle hum of the hymn, was inviting, reminiscent. . . .

"Don't tell me you're planning on cutting off that long, beautiful hair, Charlotte Tinsdale!"

"Why not? Don't you think I'll look cute in short hair? Besides, you're the best beautician in town, Katie."

"Don't try to butter me up. I've been trimming your hair since you were a little girl. You've never cut it short. Never."

"Well then, it's about time. My husband's about to be the governor of this state. I need to look like a governor's wife."

It hadn't been Pete's idea. Others had suggested, polled, questioned. . . .

"I cut my hair in 1973. Cried for a week," the lady in the chair to her left said, shaking her head. "Ended up in therapy."

"Ah, cut it," the woman to her right said. "You only live once. Besides, if you don't like it, it'll grow back."

"I have a friend who has the longest hair I've ever seen," another woman spoke up from across the room. "She's not allowed to cut it. Against her religion."

"Katie," Charlotte had argued, glaring into the mirror. "Cut it."

She did. Charlotte had cried for a week.

"Too short, Hon?" Madge placed a small mirror in the president's hand, spinning the chair so that she could have a look at the back.

"No," Charlotte said, relieved. "It's perfect."

"Well then, I guess we'd better go to work on those highlights."

"Today?" Was there really time? There was so much to do. She had to speak at a women's center.

"Can you think of a better time?" Madge argued. "Besides, what could possibly be more important than this? Who do you think you are, the president or something?"

"Very funny," Charlotte said. "You have got quite a sense of humor."

"I try."

The two women began to talk in earnest. President or not, Charlotte had missed good old-fashioned conversation. Her years in Billings might be behind her, but the friendship factor didn't have to be left behind.

"You know what I miss most?" she asked, watching Madge apply the highlighter. "I mean. . .what I really miss most about my life in Billings?"

"Tell me."

"I miss those late night dinners with Pete." Her heart twisted inside her as she spoke his name. She never talked about him anymore. It just wasn't the right thing to do—at least according to her advisors. Made the constituents uncomfortable.

"You like to cook?" Madge asked.

"Very much," Charlotte said. "But not on the nights I'm talking about. The dinners I'm talking about were Pete's favorite— fried bologna sandwiches."

"Fried bologna?"

"Yeah. He loved it. Said he grew up on it. They were too poor for ham, so he ate bologna."

"So," Madge said, "the secret is out. The president of the United States fries the best bologna in the country."

"I hate to brag," Charlotte said. "But it's true. And you know what else?"

"What, Hon?"

"I used to love to go grocery shopping. I know that sounds dumb, but it's one of the things I miss most here. I probably won't see the inside of a grocery store for the next four years."

"Pitiful. I'll think about you next time I'm standing in line at the checkout."

"And long drives in the mountains," Charlotte added, letting the sarcastic comment pass unnoticed. "I really miss that."

"Hold still, or you'll be bald headed before I'm done with you," Madge said, tugging on her hair with gloved hands.

The conversation continued on until, at last, Charlotte's hair was done. She gazed into the mirror, astounded at how different, and yet how completely natural she looked.

"What do you think, Honey?" Madge asked. "Do you like it?"

"Like it?" the president asked, reaching up to give her a hug. "I love it!"

Ashley stared, unblinking, at the unfamiliar face in the mirror.

"What do you think of the color, Honey?" her mother called out through the door that separated them.

Gazing at the reflection of short blond curls, Ashley shrugged. She couldn't help but wonder how she could ever get used to anything but the long, strawberry-colored mane she had worn all her life. However, she didn't want to hurt her mother's feelings—not after all she had gone through to spare her life. What was a change in hair color anyway?

"I've always wanted to be a blond," Ashley answered with a laugh, attempting to cover up the trembling in her voice.

She glanced in the mirror once again. How different she looked. A pair of wire-rimmed glasses sat perched atop her nose, completely nonessential, yet a necessary ingredient. A change in makeup capped off the new look. Ashley was hardly recognizable, even to herself. Not that it was bad, necessarily. . .just different.

"Hey, what's taking so long in there?" This time it was Aaron's voice.

"Uh, nothing. Nothing." Quickly touching up the lipstick, Ashley took one last look at herself in the mirror. "Ugh!" Oh well. She pushed the door open, unprepared for her mother's gasp.

"Ashley!"

"That's Brenda to you, Mother," Ashley laughed.

"How can I ever get used to calling you by another name?"

"I don't know, but I guess you'll have to."

"Well, you certainly don't look like my Ashley anyway," Mrs. Cooper said with a grin. "Turn around. Let me have a good look at you."

Ashley made a slow turn, suddenly noticing that she had caught Aaron's eye. "Well, what do you think?"

"It's. . . You look. . ."

"Go on. Say it." Suddenly she wasn't so sure she wanted to hear it.

"No. You look really good," Aaron stammered.

Ashley felt her heart flutter a little. What was it about this guy? Why did she care what he thought anyway?

Aaron wondered at the feelings that seemed to grip him as he stared at Ashley. What was it about this young woman that seemed to always take his breath away?

You look really good. The words had just slipped out, as naturally as if he had planned them. But he hadn't planned them. Where had they come from?

"Why, thank you, Sir," she responded, bowing. "I owe it all to you."

". . .and your mom," he added, looking at Angela with a smile.

They stood in silence for awhile, none daring to ask the question that still hung lingering in the air.

"What now?" Ashley asked finally.

Aaron swallowed hard. This was the tough part. It was time to get her started on the medication. There was only one place he knew of where it could be handled carefully. Aaron knew that he must find a way to transport Ashley to Havensbrook, east of the city—nearly an hour's drive away. It was dangerous, and yet. . .

"Tell me," she urged.

"I've got to send an E-mail," he answered. "Right away."

Coral paced the living room floor, peering out the front window every two or three minutes.

"What are you looking for?" Jacob asked.

"Nothing."

It was true, and yet it wasn't. She was looking for a miracle. Unfortunately, it would never be found gazing out the window.

"Coral, you've been staring out that window for an hour. You need to rest."

"Rest?" she answered angrily. "Our son is locked up at that. . . that hospital, and you say I should rest?"

How dare he? Of all people, Jacob should understand. He was supposed to be her friend, not her enemy.

"Honey, I'm just saying. . ."

"Saying what?"

"I just think you need to rest."

She did need to rest. Sleepless days and nights had passed since Jamie's arrival, but words were useless. Coral had reconciled herself to the fact that there would be no rest until her son came home. She would get him home. That much she was sure of. It didn't matter how long it took or at what cost. Her baby was coming home.

"We're going to get him," she said turning.

"What do you mean? How?"

Jacob's face showed his defeat, but she wasn't going to let it deter her. She couldn't. She wouldn't.

"We're gonna get him out of there. . .if it's the last thing we do."

TWELVE

A penny for your thoughts. . ." Mason spoke softly, hoping not to wake Abbey. She had been unusually quiet this evening, and now that everyone was down for the night, she had rolled over without much conversation.

"Hmm?" she responded groggily. "What, Honey?"

"I'm sorry, Abbey. I didn't mean to wake you." That was the last thing he wanted to do. She was exhausted. With a house full of people to take care of, she certainly deserved every precious minute of sleep. It seemed that every other minute of the day was given over to cooking, cleaning, making beds. . .

"That's fine," she said, rolling over and squeezing his hand. "Do you want to talk?"

He did want to talk. It seemed that with the house as crowded as it was, there was rarely any time for private conversation anymore. He relished their quiet moments just before dozing, when they would lie in each other's arms and reflect on the events of the day.

"You've just been so quiet tonight," he said. "I just wanted to make sure everything's okay."

"Sure. I've just been thinking. . . ."

"About Cameron?"

"How did you know?"

How did he know? He always knew. Abbey and Mason had

been married for thirty-five years. He knew her thoughts, her frustrations, her very motivations. He knew her heart.

"I've been thinking about him, too," Mason responded. "He's so different from the others."

"You mean because. . ."

She didn't finish the sentence. She didn't have to.

"No. It's not that," he said. "He just has a hardness about him that the others don't have."

"Remember June Ann?" Abbey reminded him. "When she first came? She was just like that."

"She was?"

"Yes. And old Joe Rollins had a mean streak."

"Still does," Mason muttered, trying not to laugh. The old coot had been a real handful upon arrival. Mason had all but forgotten. Perhaps he had just had time to adapt to the different personalities of his houseguests. Many had been with them for weeks now. But Cameron. . .

There was something different about him. Something that he couldn't quite put his finger on.

"I guess you're right, Honey," Mason said, yawning. "They've all changed a lot."

"Thank God," she whispered, squeezing his hand.

"Yes," he echoed, feeling both the weight of responsibility for these people and the release of knowing that they were in God's hands.

Funny, he thought, growing quiet again. . . . *Funny how life is.* He and Abbey had always wanted a large family. Circumstances had dictated otherwise. Being unable to have children of their own had seemed to be a cruel twist of fate, at least twenty years ago. But now. . .

"I love you, Mason."

Now they had a family. Now they had more family than they knew what to do with. And Aaron. . .

Well, Aaron had become a son to them during the dry years—the years of hoping, wondering, waiting. He had been

94

there when they needed him. It made perfect sense that they would be there for him now.

He needed them.

Aaron tossed and turned in the bed, sheets twisted around his ankles. He had a lot on his mind. Ashley was completely dependent on him. She would need medication, and soon. He had connections at the Cancer Research Center downtown, but was this the right time, a safe time, to approach them? And then what? He would have to drive Ashley out to Havensbrook, to Abbey and Mason's. . . .

But they had so many already. There was barely room for the "guests" he had already brought them.

How could he possibly ask for one more?

Cameron awoke to the sound of a telephone ringing. It was not unusual for Abbey and Mason to receive calls at all hours of the day and night. In fact, he should be used to it by now. But he wasn't. Every time he was awakened by the ringing, he began to shake uncontrollably.

From the other side of the house, he could hear someone coughing.

"There, there now." He heard the soft, soothing voice of Abbey, Mason's wife, as she consoled and cared for one of her houseguests.

"June Ann, is there anything I can get for you?"

Abbey's calming voice spoke out into the darkness. June Ann was, as he well knew, the only other HIV-positive case in the safe house at the moment. The young man suddenly shivered, coming to the realization that the disease was already taking its toll on her. How long would it be before it was his turn?

More coughing. And then. . .prayer. Prayer? Well, it surely sounded like prayer, anyway, not that Cameron had any fast knowledge of what a prayer should sound like. He strained to hear.

Yes. They were praying. There seemed to be a lot of that around here. Well, sick or not, he wasn't about to be pulled into any narrow-minded religious circles. Religious people had bigoted ideas about his lifestyle, his choices.

Choices. They had led him here.

Choices. None left.

It was still too dark to see the hands on his watch. Cameron pushed the button, lighting the face—4:52 A.M. Who in the world would be calling at this hour?

More whispering between Mason and Abbey piqued his curiosity, followed by the sound of the front door opening. Someone was leaving. But who? And why?

"Get out of here!" The angry voice of his father rang out from the past.

"But. . ."

"No buts, Cameron. You've disgraced our family. And don't you see what you're doing to your mother?"

He had tried to look into her eyes, but the tears were blinding. . .blinding. . .

Headlights flashed past his window, almost blinding him. The car's engine was rumbling loudly, displeased at being started at such an ungodly hour.

"Ungodly!" his father shouted loudly. "That's what your behavior is. And now you'll suffer the consequences! Just make sure you do it as far away from here as possible."

Shivering once again, Cameron rolled over in the bed, attempting to drown out the sounds of the past and present by pulling the covers up over his head. Was it going to be like this every night? Was there no rest for the weary? It was over an hour before he fell back into a fitful sleep.

"Come with us, Cameron," the voices called out. *"Say as we say. Do as we do."*

He followed blindly behind them, immersed in the dream.

"We love you, Cameron. We'll show you love. Come with us!"

"Come with you?" He took a step in their direction, the dream veering off into a direction that twisted and turned. It was a

horrible, wonderful mixture of love and lust, filling the empty places, and yet creating new ones. . . .

"*Does anyone love me?*" he called out. "*Anyone at all?*"

Bits of sunlight peeking in through the venetian blinds awakened Cameron just after dawn, the dream still tossing and turning in his head. Choosing the lifestyle had come easily. . .almost too easily.

"*Does anyone love me?*"

The words still rang in his ears.

"*Anyone at all?*"

It was still early, but Havensbrook was awake. Already there was rustling in the kitchen. Abbey must be hard at work, preparing breakfast for her guests. He had grown familiar with this routine in the three days since he had first come here. It seemed comfortable, right.

Cameron waited his turn to get into the bathroom. It was a small price to pay for his freedom, his life. Once situated, he joined the others at the breakfast table. They were no sooner seated than the door swung open. Cameron looked up to see Mason, grinning, with a young woman standing next to them.

"Cameron, this is Denise. Just arrived."

"Hey," was all Cameron could muster.

The young Asian woman stared back, looking like a scared rabbit.

What are you looking at? Cameron wanted to say, but didn't. He was, instead, struck by a moment of conscience, remembering his first moments at Havensbrook just a few days earlier. How alone he had felt. How frightened.

No, he mustn't treat this one like a stranger—or be intimidated by her. This was another boarder, another friend.

"It's good to meet you," Cameron said, sticking out his hand. "My name is Cameron."

Ashley turned to look Aaron squarely in the eye. "Are you always in such a good mood?" she asked.

"I try to be."

"I find it annoying." She did, though she couldn't explain why. How could anyone be in such a good mood all the time? It was irritating.

"Sorry." He shrugged, suddenly looking more like a helpless kitten than a heroic knight in shining armor.

Only the third day into her new role, Ashley was already tired of the secrecy and was rapidly tiring of pretending to be someone she wasn't. She was claustrophobic, wearied by the idea of staying cooped up here in Aaron's tiny West Houston apartment. The days seemed to drag by, this one worse than the ones before. She had been through four television shows, three meals, and one novel, and it was only early evening.

Aaron had been very good about everything—almost too good. He had given up the bed in this tiny one-bedroom apartment so that she could be comfortable. He had slept on the couch without complaint. He had cooked meals, washed dishes, and done the laundry. All in all, he was a perfect gentleman. That was almost enough to make up for the sparsely decorated, somewhat messy apartment and the wrinkled lab coat he always wore.

Almost.

Hours had turned into days, and enough was enough. She wanted, more than anything, to just go home and let life get back to normal. She wanted to go to work. She wanted to call her friends. She wanted to. . .to have a life. But that wouldn't happen—not now, maybe not ever.

And this man—the one who had chatted her ear off the first day here, had hardly spoken a word since. It wasn't that he wasn't nice. He was. Very. But he seemed to be completely lost in his own world, his own "cause."

She shook her head, trying to remind herself that their "causes" had now overlapped. He had, after all, risked his life to save her.

He could keep his good mood. None of this was any fun to Ashley.

"Isn't there something we can do?" she asked for the ump-teenth time.

"Like what?"

"Go out for pizza or a movie maybe. I don't know."

"You do know," Aaron answered firmly. "We can't go any-where—not yet, anyway. I could rent some more movies."

"*Sense and Sensibility?*"

Aaron groaned loudly.

"What?" she asked defiantly. It was her favorite.

"It's just. . ."

"What?"

"Never mind," Aaron said. "Anything else?"

"Can I use your mobile to call my mom?" Ashley asked.

"You've already talked to her twelve times today," came his abrupt reply, "but if you feel like you've got any more words left in you, go ahead."

She rolled her eyes again. "You know," she said, "just because men don't know how to talk doesn't mean that women don't."

"Who said I don't know how to talk?"

"You've barely said two words since I got here," she muttered.

"Slight exaggeration."

"Only slight," she said, staring.

"Okay. You want to talk?" he asked, leaning back against the chair. "I'm all ears."

Yeah, he was all ears all right. They were as big as boats—and almost as big as that nose he carried around with him everywhere he went.

"Why do I have to be the one to do the talking?" she asked. "What about you?"

"What about me?"

"Well," she said, her voice snapping, "for one thing. . .do you ever speak in more than three-word sentences?"

"Yeah."

"I rest my case."

"I do know how to talk, Ashley," Aaron said suddenly, taking her by surprise. "I just don't open up and talk to anyone and everyone. I'm not like that."

"Well, I'm not either," she said, feeling herself relax a little. She dropped down onto the arm of the couch, looking at him curiously. "I don't have a lot of friends."

That was true, though she hated to admit it. She was a mover and shaker—but, like other movers and shakers, she always seemed to shake off any potential relationships simply by virtue of her busyness.

"I have friends," he said, though he seemed to be choosing his words carefully. "But I guess you could say I'm not terribly social. I'm too busy with the movement."

"So how did you get involved in this intervention group, or whatever you call it?" Ashley asked. "I mean. . .I know what you told me about the government and your convictions and all that, but how did you get involved? And when?"

She couldn't help but notice his eyes shift downward. He bit his lip, not saying anything for a moment.

"Well?"

"I, uh," he stammered. "I guess I really got involved three years ago when my parents died."

"Oh." Ashley suddenly felt as if she had treaded into a forbidden zone. Perhaps it would be best to back out.

Fortunately, Aaron took care of that for her. "I've got to check my E-mail," he said, standing suddenly. "That's six words—seven if you count E-mail as two words."

"Very funny."

"I try."

"Why do you have to check your E-mail?" Ashley asked. "You've already checked it twenty times today."

"Another exaggeration. . ."

"Really. Why?"

"I'm expecting a letter from someone," Aaron said, suddenly serious.

"Who?"

"I guess it's okay to tell you," Aaron responded. "His name is Mason Wallis. He and his wife run a safe house."

"A safe house? Where?"

"East of here. About an hour."

"Is this what you do?" she asked. "I mean, you rescue people, then drive them to these safe houses?"

"Basically."

"So I guess I'm just one in a list of beautiful women you've done this for?"

Okay, so maybe the word beautiful could have been left out. . . . It was really more of an accusation than a question anyway.

Aaron shrugged, grinning. "Beautiful? That might be stretching it a little, don't you think?"

Ashley glared at him.

"What?" he stammered. "Oh, I didn't mean that you aren't beautiful. I just—"

"Forget it. How did you meet this guy anyway?" she asked smugly.

"He was my Sunday school teacher when I was a kid," Aaron said, grinning. "He's actually the one who got me involved in the. . .well, the movement."

"Sunday school? You were a church kid?" she asked, astonished.

"Yeah. Still am."

Oh, brother. Well, that explained his Mister Nice Guy image.

"Not me. I tried it a couple of times when my aunt Sharon would drag me to her church, but religion was not for me."

"Religion is not for anyone," he answered with a knowing look.

She rolled her eyes, looking back. *What in the world was that supposed to mean?*

Fear gripped Shannon as she stood outside the door of apartment 312, preparing to knock. She hadn't seen her younger brother in ages. They certainly weren't what anyone would call close. But whom else could she turn to? She had already spent all afternoon driving around in circles, trying to think. . .trying to decide. . .

But Aaron? Their last words had been anything but civil. Just hours after their parents' funeral, and she had blasted him, accused him. . .

"Where were you? You were supposed to be here!"

She tried to push the words from her mind. Would he even speak to her now? Where else could she go?

Shannon was exhausted. The kids were exhausted. And Frank. . . Well, by now, Frank was probably making phone calls to every friend she had, trying to locate her. One thing was for sure—he would never think of calling here.

Her brother was, and always had been, a young man of great conviction. That was, in part, why Shannon had stayed away from him for months at a time. He was so, so. . .narrow-minded. But perhaps, just perhaps that's why she felt she needed him so much now.

She stood, tentatively, working up the courage to knock.

"Do something!"

She knocked lightly.

Aaron's heart skipped a nervous beat, hearing the rap on the door. "Who is that?" he whispered.

"Are you expecting someone?" Ashley whispered, taking small steps backward.

Aaron shook his head. No, he wasn't. His only potential contact was to be made via E-mail. The rapping continued, followed by a bark. Was that a dog? Someone was here—with a dog? Did he dare answer it? His heart picked up speed.

Aaron motioned with his head for Ashley to go to the back bedroom. She moved quickly, quietly, closing the door behind her. He walked on eggshells toward the front door, peeking through the hole to try to catch a glimpse of his visitor before swinging the door open.

For heaven's sake. . .

Shannon. His older sister. He hadn't seen her in ages.

"Do something! Don't just stand there!"

What in the world was she doing here now? Beside her—Veronica, holding a puppy, and little Zachary. Something must be wrong, terribly wrong, for them to have come here.

"Do something!"

Glancing back toward the bedroom door, Aaron took a deep breath. He had no choice. He had to let them in.

THIRTEEN

Shannon felt her heart begin to race as the door opened. There before her stood Aaron—the brother she scarcely knew.

"Shannon? . . ."

"Aaron." The tears came quickly. "Can I come in?"

"Of course." He ushered her into the apartment, away from any wandering eyes.

She heard the door click behind her and gently nudged the children toward this unfamiliar uncle for an equally uncomfortable hug.

"Are you okay?" Aaron asked, looking her in the eye.

"No. I'm not okay." She felt her eyes drift to the floor, unable to accept his gaze. Her heart was pounding madly.

"Do something!"

He gestured for her to sit. "What's going on?"

"I, uh. . .I need to talk to you about something."

The children joined her, pressing to her like chicks to a mother hen. She could feel their fear. *This is so unfair to them,* Shannon thought, pulling Veronica and Zachary even closer.

"Tell me, Shannon," Aaron urged.

"It's, um. . .something. . .private," she said, brushing the tears off her cheek. "Is there a place where the kids can. . .can. . .play or something?"

"I've got a TV in the bedroom."

Aaron could have slapped himself silly. No sooner were the words out than he realized what he had done.

"I mean. . ."

"No, TV's fine," Shannon assured him.

Aaron stood, eyes darting quickly toward the bedroom door. How could he let them in there? Ashley was in there.

"I can do it!" Veronica said, throwing the door to the bedroom open.

Aaron gasped. Surely everything was about to unravel. A few anxious seconds went by—silent seconds. He stepped tentatively toward the bedroom. It was empty, painfully empty. Where in the world was Ashley?

"What can we watch?" Veronica asked, tugging on his arm.

"Uh, I've got some movies—right there," Aaron said hesitantly, pointing to a stack of videos.

His eyes scoured the room. Where had Ashley gone? Into the bathroom? The closet? Under the bed?

"What movie?" Veronica asked, tugging harder.

"Look, what about this one?" Shannon asked, making a selection. "Now you two settle down and watch this so Uncle Aaron and I can talk." She popped the video into the VCR.

"Okay Mommy, but I'm sleepy."

"You can climb up on the bed," Aaron said, pointing.

He breathed a sigh of relief as the kids settled onto the bed, Gilligan nuzzled between them. So far, so good. Closing the door to the bedroom, Shannon turned to face him. Aaron was hardly prepared for what she was about to say.

Ashley heard the chatter of the children outside the closet door but couldn't make out what they were saying. Who were they? Did Aaron have children? Was he married? He had never mentioned a wife, let alone kids.

She sat some time in silence, straining to hear something. . . anything. Was that a bark? Nah, surely she was imagining things.

Come on guys. I'm getting sleepy in here. . . .

She was unaware of the time that passed as her eyes grew heavier. She began to drift off, carried away by her thoughts and dreams.

Aaron's heart almost came to a stop when he heard the children cry out. "Mommy! Mommy!"

They came running like banshees from the bedroom, squealing all the way.

"What is it?" Shannon's face turned white as she voiced the question.

Aaron tried to prepare himself for the inevitable, though even he could not have been more surprised by Veronica's words. "There's a strange lady snoring in the closet!"

Aaron felt his face redden immediately. The look on his sister's face was quite a sight. She was obviously confused.

"What did you say?" Shannon asked the kids, apparently not understanding.

"Come on, Mom—I'll show you."

Aaron, trying to look as innocent as possible, padded along behind the trio. He did everything he could to avoid Shannon's stares as the children pulled her into the bedroom. They were no sooner in the door than the sound of snoring met them.

"What in the world? . . ." Shannon asked.

Aaron shrugged, feeling his heartbeat pick up speed. The sound led them to the closet—his closet. There, tucked away in the corner, pressed against the wall, lay Ashley Cooper, snoring loudly. She looked hysterical. She looked. . .adorable. Yes, she looked adorable. Standing there, taken in by the humor of the moment, Aaron found himself thinking the unthinkable.

"Who is she?" little Veronica asked, whispering loudly.

"Uh. . ."

"Yes, Aaron—who is she?" Shannon asked with a grin. "Is there something we should know. . .or should I say *someone* we should know? . . ."

"She's a. . .a. . ."

"I can see what she is," Shannon said with a smirk. "Who is she?"

"Uncle Aaron's got a girlfriend! Uncle Aaron's got a girlfriend!" Veronica began to chant.

Horrified, Aaron realized that Ashley was stirring. "No, Honey—shhh. . ." But it was too late—far too late.

Ashley awoke to the strangest noise—the laughter of a child. At least, it sounded like a child. But, where was she? She felt so disoriented. Something cold and wet was licking her nose. What in the world? . . .

A puppy? Aaron didn't have a puppy. Ashley shook her head, trying to arouse herself. It was taking a few seconds for her to get her bearings. Oh yes, she was hidden in Aaron's bedroom closet—all alone.

Okay, not quite alone. . . Looking up, she was shocked to find an enthusiastic audience. Ten wondering eyes stared down at her. Two of them were recognizable. Two belonged to the puppy. The others were new.

She looked intently back at them, her heart beginning to race. *Oh no.* . . What should she do? Were these people here to hurt her?

No, two of them were just children—laughing children. But were they. . .were they Aaron's children?

"Uh, hello," she whispered, finally.

Scrambling, she made her way to her feet, her eyes fixed on Aaron's. He looked pale, nervous.

Who is that woman? Ashley wondered, looking at Shannon out of the corner of her eye. She was pretty. A twinge of jealousy shot through her. What in the world was that all about? She certainly had no claim to this man.

Aaron suddenly felt like a schoolboy accused of cheating on his spelling test. What should he do? He looked back and forth between the two ladies, wondering, worrying—knowing that he'd better say something soon—or suffer the consequences. There was only one thing he could do. And considering Shannon's news, the truth was bound to come out anyway.

"Let's go in the living room," he said, reaching out to help Ashley, who still looked a little out of sorts.

With newfound confidence, he led everyone back to the living room, where proper introductions were quickly made. The children then returned to the bedroom to watch TV so that Aaron and the two women could talk.

And talk they did—for over an hour, sharing their intimate stories, getting to know each other.

"Just what the doctor ordered," Aaron whispered to himself, looking at Ashley. She was chattering like a kid on a playground. She was headlong into a story, with a grin covering her face. It was the first time he had seen her really happy in days.

And Shannon. . . Well, that was another story indeed. Aaron stared at his sister. She had changed a lot in just a couple of years. He couldn't help but notice the lines of aging around her eyes. They were young eyes. Why did they bear the strain of an older woman?

"Do something!"

He shook the awful words from his mind, just as a special news bulletin came on the television in the bedroom. At 8:05 P.M. central time their new president, Charlotte Tinsdale, was going to address the nation.

FOURTEEN

Charlotte Tinsdale trembled as she faced the television camera. Still new in office, she hadn't quite gotten used to the idea of addressing the country as its leader. There seemed to be a haze of unreality that hung about her in moments like this. Could this really be happening? Was it just a dream?

No, it was reality. The proof was just off in the distance, about twenty feet or so. There, to her right, stood her two sons, cheering her on. They were her refuge, her reason for pushing forward every day, whether she felt like it or not.

"My fellow Americans," she began, her heart racing.

What was she supposed to say next? Ah yes, the Teleprompter. It provided the reassurance she needed. Charlotte read the words almost rhythmically, trying to keep herself focused. It wasn't easy.

This was a fairly typical state of the union address—or was it? Ironically, it was the state of the union that bothered Charlotte right now. Nothing was as it should be—in the legislature, in the courts, in the White House. Overwhelmed by it all, President Charlotte Tinsdale was having a hard time making things right. Her dream of fixing everything seemed almost futile now.

It seemed to be playing itself out in the form of nightmares. Ever since her move to the White House, she had been plagued by horrible dreams. In them, corpses all cried out to her from beyond the grave. Last night's was the worst of all. Her husband, Pete, was lying on his deathbed, pleading for mercy as lawmakers' poison dripped into his veins. His cries were terrifying.

She shivered, remembering how real, how awful it had been. Focusing, she continued to read the words from the faithful Teleprompter.

"Our hopes, our dreams as a nation. . ."

She spoke the words, but her mind was elsewhere. She found herself caught up in the dream again. . . .

Pete was calling her by name, begging for her to stop the IV. She wanted to, but seemed to be frozen in place. She couldn't make the necessary steps to get to his bed—her feet frozen, her hands tied by lawmakers. He was dying. . .dying. . .

But that wasn't how Pete died, Charlotte reminded herself, trying to get a grip. He had been killed in a small plane crash while on a goodwill trip to South America four years ago.

"Do something!"

What could she do? His lifeless body was hundreds of miles away. . . .

Pete wasn't even alive when the Duty to Die law was passed by Congress. He would have opposed it, of course, as she now did—but what could she do? Her hands were tied. All of these years she had hoped, prayed that she would find herself where she now stood. And yet here she stood, a widow, hands tied behind her back because of a law that she hadn't been responsible for and couldn't do anything about. This wasn't the way it was supposed to be.

"Do something!"

What can I. . . What can anyone do? The words, just a whisper of a thought, caused a momentary pause in the speech.

Charlotte managed to continue, now speaking with conviction: "In regard to the issue at hand, this new way of thinking. . . Some would call it sensible. I'm not so sure about that. It's almost too pragmatic, too practical. The human factor has been left out. And now we're headed down a road to. . .to who knows where."

She was off the Teleprompter now but didn't care. The

speechwriters would just have to get over it. She had some important issues to discuss with those who had put her in office. It was for them she spoke.

"I find myself troubled by the apparent lack of respect for human life. We have to begin to look for new ways to deal with the tough situations that we face. We have a choice. We can either work on eliminating the problems themselves—the diseases, the birth defects, the results of overpopulation—or we can choose to eliminate those who have the audacity to inconvenience us by getting in our way."

Boy, was she off the Teleprompter. But still she continued on, unashamed, courageous. . .

"Euthanizing them seems so. . .practical, at least to some. But what happens when we kill them off—one million, two, three—and discover that the problems remain? What if we get somewhere down the road and realize we made a wrong turn back at the fork in the road? Will there be any turning back for us then? This is the question that haunts me. Can we possibly undo what we've done? . . . Isn't there something we can do?"

"Do something!"

Feeling the eyes of the cameraman bearing down on her, Charlotte began to panic. She also felt the familiar knot in her throat and realized she was about to cry—but she couldn't, not here, not in front of the press and the American people. She forced herself to speak a few remaining words, then quickly concluded.

But it wasn't over. The most difficult part lay ahead. She turned to face the onslaught of reporters, their questions sending her reeling. For a moment Charlotte Tinsdale couldn't even remember her own name, let alone what she was doing standing here facing the world all alone.

Shannon turned to face the others in the room, tears streaming down her face. "Thank God," she whispered. "Thank God."

Reaching out, she embraced Aaron, the brother she had barely known. They were in this thing together—and now maybe they weren't alone. Maybe someone was on their side—someone in a high place.

Frank dialed the number angrily.

"Paul?"

"Yeah, Frank?"

"Did you hear that?"

"Sure. I heard it," Paul said nonchalantly. "What else did you expect? I told you from the beginning she was going to be trouble. She's too vulnerable. Doesn't have the necessary backbone."

"No. If I recall—I told you that," Frank argued.

"What's the difference?"

It didn't matter, and Frank certainly didn't feel like arguing. Right now they needed to stick together. It looked as if they suddenly found themselves facing a formidable enemy—one in heels and a skirt.

"What's the story with Jerome Patterson?" Frank asked.

"The P.I.? I think he's tracking an intervention group working out of the medical center here in Houston. Why?"

"Oh, no reason. I just wondered."

He wondered, all right. Wondered where his wife was, what she was doing. Wondered if he would ever see his children again. More importantly, wondered whom else she had told.

Aaron met his sister's embrace with waves of guilt and overwhelming relief. Was it possible? Had she finally forgiven him?

Hannah reached out to grab the remote control from the coffee table, hoping to snap off the television before the reporters had a chance to dissect the president's words. And what words they had been!

Do you see, Sister?!?! she wanted to scream. *There is someone on our side.*

But, then again, she already knew that. There was someone on their side—someone in a much higher position than the presidency of the United States. When would someone begin to tell that story?

Coral turned off the television, heading straight for the computer.

"There's got to be something I can do," she muttered, her thoughts still focused on what Charlotte Tinsdale had just said, ". . .someone I can tell."

How many people had heard the story already—and yet none had the power, the authority, to change the situation? Who could? Who would?

Just that morning Coral had visited the baby again. She had watched in anger as the doctors inserted a small microchip under the skin of his right hand. It was customary for infants in this "position," she had been told. Coral had run her finger over the tiny stitches lovingly, angrily.

What gave them the right? Jamie was a precious baby. He was her baby. There was no law higher than that—at least, not in her eyes. What right did they have to do as they pleased with him?

Of course, she understood their logic. That's what made her angriest of all. Now her hopes of stealing the baby away from Mercy Hospital were slimmer than ever.

She snapped the computer on angrily. "Come on, come on!" she muttered, watching it boot up.

The familiar screen made its appearance, and Coral began to type frantically. She signed onto the Internet, quickly typing in the words "Duty to Die."

Coral had no idea what she was looking for. She was just looking for anyone, anything that might help save her son.

FIFTEEN

Aaron pulled the car out onto the dark interstate. Traffic was slow this time of night, even for Houston's Southwest Freeway. He slipped in between a new Mustang and an older Cadillac, easing his way into the flow of the highway. It was just a matter of time now, and everything would come together. Just one more transaction to take care of. . .

One car to trade. One drive to make. One drop-off to complete. He had done this dozens of times. Why did tonight seem so extraordinary?

He glanced into the rearview mirror, trying to catch a glimpse of Shannon and the kids. This was special because they were special. . . .

"Everyone okay back there?"

"Uh huh," Shannon answered.

"Yes!" Veronica shouted, jumping up and scaring the daylights out of him.

"Put your seatbelt back on!" he warned. "Don't make me pull this car over."

She settled back into her seat, and he heard the snap of the belt as it was fastened. Her tiny voice was a reminder of the life that he had not yet lived—the lack of family, lack of children. . . Would he ever find the one person who was meant for him?

Almost instinctively, Aaron looked out of the corner of his

eye at the young woman next to him. Ashley was cute with the blond curls, he had to admit.

"Snap out of it, Man," he whispered to himself.

Quietly, he surveyed the group. This trip to Gilead might not be so bad after all.

"How much farther?" Ashley asked, straining to look out the window of the Jeep. It was too dark to see where they were going. Traveling at night might have been a necessity, a safety precaution—but it sure wasn't very scenic.

"Yeah, how long, Uncle Aaron?" Veronica chimed in, yawning. "We've been in the car forever."

"We've only been in the car a few minutes," Aaron said with a laugh. "It just seems like forever."

Ashley looked over at him. He looked so relaxed behind the wheel, headed to who-knows-where. Someplace east of the city was all he would tell her. She sure hoped he knew what he was doing. But they had come this far together, hadn't they?

"Where are we going exactly?" she asked hesitantly.

"Dairy Queen on Chambers."

"Ice cream!" Veronica yelled out.

"No, Honey. Dairy Queen is already closed," he answered, grinning.

"Then why are we going there?" she asked innocently.

"Yes, why are we going there?" Shannon chimed in.

"We'll trade cars and head on out."

"And then? . . ."

"Then we finish the drive to Havensbrook."

"Havensbrook." It sounded like a fancy name for a mental institution.

"I sure hope you know what you're doing," Ashley mumbled.

"I'd like to think I do," he answered.

"Of course, I don't want you to think I don't trust you just because of that shocking red hair," she said, jokingly. "I used to be a redhead myself."

"It's blond."

"Please."

Ashley laid her head back, relaxing. It was more blond than red, but she had enjoyed teasing him about it for the last few days.

Aaron snapped on the radio. Country gospel.

Not again. Ashley groaned as loudly as she could. "Just shoot me now," she mumbled.

"What?"

"Nothing." It wasn't worth arguing about. "I just don't like making all these stops and starts," she said. "It's not like my life isn't in enough danger already, you know."

"Yes, Ashley. I do know."

True. He was the one who had rescued her, come to think of it.

Flashing lights of a patrol car appeared behind them. Ashley's heart began to race, nearly leaping from her chest. *Oh no!* It couldn't end like this! Not after all she had been through!

Aaron slowed the car down a bit, pulling off to the side of the road. The patrol car sped on by in pursuit of another vehicle.

Ashley's breathing slowed, though her hands were still shaking uncontrollably. "Thank God," she muttered.

"Thank who?" Aaron asked, grinning at her.

"Never mind." It was just a slip.

"Dairy Queen! Dairy Queen!" Veronica's shrill, tiny voice cut through her, startling her back to reality.

The parking lot was dark. The restaurant was closed for the night.

A flicker of headlights. . .once, twice, three times. Was it a signal?

"I've come that you might have life."

They heard the voice, though faintly. Who was it? What did it mean?

"I've come that you might have life."

This was a voice to be trusted. Quietly, carefully, the switch was made.

"I've come that you might have life. . . ."

Shannon couldn't even let the words pass through her mind without wondering about the baby she carried. Was it a boy or a girl? Another little girl would be so much fun for Veronica—a little sister! But Frank would love another son. . . .

Frank.

He wouldn't love another son. He had made it plain. He wouldn't love another child, regardless. He wouldn't tolerate another child. . . .

Shannon's mind began to wander. Where was Frank? What was he doing? Was he missing them? Was he looking for them? A tear worked its way down her cheek. She quickly brushed it away.

Frank paced back and forth across the kitchen. Dishes were starting to pile up in the sink—a clear indication that Shannon was gone.

"Where in blue blazes is she?" he muttered, looking out of the window, half expecting her to walk up the driveway as she had done a thousand times before.

Tick, tick, tick. . .

The clock beckoned him. 10:42.

Tick, tick, tick. . .

It was the only sound in the room, and it was really beginning to irritate him.

Focus, Blaine—focus!

Dr. Blaine Bishop tried to force himself to look at the computer screen. He was trying to balance his checking account, but it didn't seem to be working. Nothing seemed to be working.

All he could think about—all he could see—were dead bodies. Everywhere he turned—more dead bodies. They were there in his sleep. They were there in his daydreams. They were there every time he turned on the television.

Tick, tick, tick. . .

Was it the clock, or the sound of his own heart beating? It was getting harder to tell these days.

Tick, tick, tick. . .

He looked down at the computer screen. 10:50 P.M. He should be headed to bed. After all, he had to get up early in the morning, had to. . .

He didn't want to think about what he had to do the following morning. It was always the same, day after day. One "patient" after another. They were all alike.

"I can't take the pain!"

"Please, not that! Not again!"

"You know what to do!" his wife cried out, anguished. *"Just do it!"*

But he couldn't, he wouldn't. . . . She was more than just a patient, more than a nameless face.

No, they weren't all alike.

And that girl—that Ashley Cooper—why couldn't he get her off of his mind? There was nothing unique about her, after all. She was just another "patient" in a long line of patients. So she hadn't been given all the facts, so what? There had been plenty of others before her. There would be plenty of others after.

Frustrated, Blaine turned his attention back to the computer screen. It was no use. He wasn't going to get any work done tonight at all.

Hannah tossed and turned in the bed. She couldn't seem to get her recent conversation with Molly out of her mind. Frustrated, she reached over to flip on the light.

"What are you doing in there?" She heard her sister's voice through the thin bedroom wall.

"Nothing. Just couldn't sleep, that's all." That was an understatement. "Go back to sleep."

Silence.

Hannah reached to pick up her Bible from the bedside table. Somehow, somewhere there must be an answer. She was going to find it, if it took all night. She thumbed her way through the familiar book until she found the Scripture she had been looking for. . . .

"I have come that they may have life, and have it to the full."

Placing the Bible back on the bedside table, she turned her attention to prayer.

Sixteen

Found anything?"

Coral looked up from the computer screen, eyes stinging, to face Jacob. He looked as tired as she felt.

"Sort of," she responded. "There's a lot of information circulated about the new law—from both sides of the fence."

"Show me," he said, sitting next to her.

Coral looked at him closely, suddenly realizing that she hadn't even spoken more than two or three words to him in days. This man was her husband, her soul mate—and she had shut him out.

"Are you sure?" she asked, placing her hand in his.

He nodded, giving it a squeeze.

"Well. . ." She backed her way into a previous page. "This one is interesting. It seems there is a group of congressmen who have been vocally opposed to the law. They're looking at ways to. . .I don't know—what would you call it? Overturn it? Overrule it?"

Jacob shrugged. "I'm no lawyer. I sure don't know how these things work. I just want my son back."

"Me too. But the interesting thing is, some of them are in the same boat we are. . . ." She pointed to the screen. "Look at these stories. People everywhere are trying to save their loved ones. This one congressman has a niece with. . .what does it say?"

"Leukemia."

"Yeah, look here. . . . He's filed an. . .an injunction."

Coral looked up at Jacob with hope.

"He filed an injunction," she whispered, her eyes gleaming for the first time in days.

"What does that mean?"

A little more searching brought the necessary answer. . . . "It's a legal action that keeps someone from carrying out an action."

"Keeps them from doing it?" Jacob echoed. "How?"

"Let's see," she said, reading down the web page. "The purpose of an injunction is to 'hold things steady' until the trial. Then a final judgment will be made."

"How do we do it?" he asked, pulling up a chair.

Coral shrugged, not wanting to let herself feel hope. "I don't know," she said. "But maybe that congressman does."

Ashley yawned, looking out of the window into the darkness of the country road. Even in the dark she could tell they were in the piney woods of East Texas. The blackness seemed to almost swallow them up, whizzing by in the shadows of oncoming headlights.

"So, where is this Havensbrook, anyway?" she asked, turning her attention back to those in the car.

"Just outside of Gilead," Aaron answered. "We're almost there now."

"Gilead." She let the word roll across her tongue. Why did it sound so familiar? It was a soothing word, a peaceful word.

"Gilead." Zachary squealed the word with a twist that only a two year old could put on it.

"Not so loud, Zachary!" Shannon said, trying to quiet him.

"We're almost there, Buddy," Aaron assured him. "Maybe another five, ten minutes."

"Then what?" Ashley asked, nervously.

What will happen when we reach this safe house? Is it really as safe as Aaron lets on? The last thing she wanted was to find herself in an even worse situation.

"Then you stay awhile."

"How long?"

"I wish I could answer that," he said kindly. "But I really don't know."

"I miss my mom," she said, feeling her heart swell already.

"You just saw her today."

"I know, but. . ."

"What?"

"We're very close, that's all. Can. . .can she come and see me?" The thought of being away from her mom for more than a few days really tore at her. Ever since her father's death, she and her mother had been closer than ever.

"Probably. But I'm sure it's just a matter of time before the police begin tracking her. They may have started already."

Those words sent a shock wave through her.

"Why?" But she knew why. Everyone had already risked so much. . .for her. That was the real why question. . . .

Looking up at Aaron once again, Ashley let her mind wander. Why was he so interested in helping her? It wasn't for money —he hadn't taken any of that—not even from her mother. No, he must have had his reasons. But what were they?

He seemed to be a really nice guy—a really good guy. But what was so good about him? Was it the fact that he helped people, or was there something more to it than that? He seemed to really care—on a deeper level than most people. He seemed so. . . extraordinary. And what was all that stuff about being a Sunday school kid? He sure didn't look like the religious type.

Ashley looked at him a little closer. Okay, so his nose was a little big, so what? Looks weren't everything.

Hold it, Girl! What in the world are you thinking? She shocked herself back to reality. What was she doing thinking about Aaron like that? The absolute last thing she needed in her life right now was a man, and the absolute last man on earth she would consider was someone like Aaron. He was just too. . .innocent. She had always dated the brassy ones, not the nice guys.

The puppy barked unexpectedly. Ashley turned around to catch a glimpse and got a wet lick across her cheek instead.

"Gilligan, stop that!" Shannon said, pulling him back.

Ashley smiled. She didn't mind—not really. In fact, it was the first kiss she had received in quite awhile.

Shannon pulled the puppy off of Ashley, irritated. This was turning out to be a long, aggravating night. She sat quietly, listening to Aaron and Ashley talk. These two were either going to be mortal enemies or end up married; she couldn't decide which. The very thought sent a sudden jealous streak through her. If she couldn't be happy, no one could be happy.

"That's stupid," she muttered, resolved to change her mood before it changed her.

She ran her fingers through Zachary's hair with one hand, slipping the other arm around Veronica.

"I love you guys," she said quietly. "Do you know that?"

The children nodded. Shannon smiled. It was all the answer she needed to keep her going. They were the reason for her existence right now, whether they knew it or not.

Her thoughts began to shift to her brother Aaron, to the break in their relationship, to the night—a night not unlike tonight, really—when everything had changed for both of them.

Do something!

It had started like many other nights in her young life—an invitation to dinner at their parents' house, just miles north of Houston in The Woodlands. She and Frank would be there, with Veronica, just turned three. They were to arrive at eight o'clock. Aaron was expected at 7:45—a special petition from his mother, who had requested his help with the sauce for the grilled chicken fettuccine, his specialty.

She had no way of knowing that Aaron wouldn't be there. She had no way of knowing that her mother and father would be. . .

No! No!

Shannon pushed away angry tears, catching a glimpse of her younger brother in the rearview mirror.

Where were you? she wanted to cry out, even now. *You were never late!*

"They should be here by now," Mason said, looking at his watch. "Aaron is never late."

"Don't worry, Honey," Abbey spoke quietly, handing him a cup of coffee. "It's only 11:30. It's not so late. Besides, it's in the Lord's hands."

"I know." Mason seated himself at the head of the kitchen table, waiting for the familiar shimmer of headlights through the window. His other houseguests were, for the most part, already settled in for the evening. He and Abbey would have already turned in themselves if they had not been awaiting the arrival of Aaron and his family.

Mason's mind shot back in time. He was just a young married man at the time, teaching a fifth-grade Sunday school class. One student in particular was giving him fits—a rough-looking rich kid by the name of Aaron Landers. He was loud, disruptive, and, well, basically obnoxious in every way.

"Would you like to come to the front of the class and tell everyone what's so funny?" Mason had asked him aloud one Sunday morning. It was a Sunday he would never forget.

"Uh, I. . . ," Aaron had answered at first.

Mason had watched as the youngster fought for words. Slowly Aaron had stood, making his way to the front of the class.

"Speak up, young man," Mason had said, staring at him sternly. "What's so funny?"

For a moment nothing happened. And then, almost before he had time to catch his breath, Aaron had pulled a huge green bullfrog out of his pocket. It leaped from his hands, smacking Mason squarely in the face.

The entire class had fallen apart. Had it not been for Mason's sense of humor, the whole thing might have turned terribly ugly. But he had simply picked the frog up, examined it carefully, and thanked Aaron Landers for his upcoming lunch.

The look on the youngster's face had been worth it all.

And now, more than twenty years later, he couldn't help but look back on that day and smile—not for the frog who had been carefully placed into the backyard upon arriving home, but for the youngster. . .the little obnoxious one—the one into whom he had immediately determined to invest time and energy on that particular morning.

He had never regretted one moment of it. And on a night just three years ago, Aaron had needed him like never before. Mason had once again invested time and energy into the young man—a young man who had still turned out to be a troublemaker—in his own special sort of way.

Leaning back in his chair, Mason looked at his watch again—11:33.

No, Aaron was never late.

"This is it," Aaron said, pulling the car off the road. His heart began to beat a little faster in anticipation of their arrival. Coming to Havensbrook always made him feel better about things. There was something so special, so peaceful about this place.

"This doesn't even look like a road," Ashley said, sounding nervous.

"It's okay. I've done this dozens of times."

He had, too. Many times over the last few months he had made this trip, planning, transporting—bringing food, supplies. But tonight's cargo seemed more precious than before. Tonight he was about to deliver his sister and her children over to Mason Wallis.

His sister. . .

Aaron looked in the rearview mirror, catching a glimpse of Shannon, now sleeping soundly, a child pressed to each shoulder. There was so much still left unsaid between them—so much that needed to be resolved, understood. Would there be time? No, he must drop them off at Mason's and then. . .

Mason Wallis. . . He couldn't help but think about the old guy and grin. Mason had certainly taught him a thing or two in Sunday school over the years. He had been quite a teacher. Rephrase that. He still was quite a teacher. Barely a week went by that Aaron didn't learn something of life from Mason Wallis.

He turned the car onto a small dirt lane, trees framing both sides casting shadowy images down into the car.

"I'm scared," Veronica cried from the back seat.

"It's okay, Babe," Aaron said. "We're almost there now."

He focused on what little he could see of the road. Ah, there it was in the distance. . .the house.

Havensbrook. They were home at last.

SEVENTEEN

Mom, I don't feel good."

President Charlotte Tinsdale looked down into the face of her eleven-year-old son Jonathan and smiled.

"Tell the truth!" she said with a laugh. "You just don't want to start a new school tomorrow."

It was going to be a big day, a big challenge—but certainly no bigger than the challenges he had already faced over the last few days.

"No, Mom," he argued. "I really don't feel good. I have a headache and my stomach aches. I feel like I'm gonna faint."

"You're so dramatic."

"No, really, Mom."

Maybe he wasn't playing around. She reached out to feel his head. He did feel a little warm. "How about some Tylenol?"

"They gave me some earlier."

"Who?" Charlotte still couldn't get used to living in a house filled with people.

"One of those ladies. I don't know," he mumbled, looking down. "Anyway, I took some about two hours ago. It didn't help."

This wasn't like him, Charlotte had to admit. Of course, a lot had happened over the last few days. As leader of the nation, she had had little time to be leader of the home. Maybe Jonathan was just feeling the effects of all that had happened. Well, she was about to assume a leadership role now.

"Okay, I'll make you a deal," she said, looking him in the eye. "You can stay home on one condition. . ."

"What?"

"You spend the day with me!" she said, taking him by the hand.

President or not, there were more important matters to tend to here.

Frank pulled open the pantry door, digging around for something that looked like breakfast.

"Shannon, aren't you going to go to the—?"

He stopped short, remembering. Shannon wasn't here. He fumbled around through half-eaten boxes of cereal, finally deciding on some Froot Loops.

"Where's the? . . ." He reached inside the fridge for the milk. What he came up with looked a little more like cottage cheese. "I don't believe this!"

Angrily, he pulled his jacket on. He lit a cigarette, took a long drag, and looked around the room.

Empty.

A long fit of coughing took him by surprise.

"NickStop. . .stops the craving before it begins."

Grabbing his briefcase, Frank headed for the door. He had enough to worry about today without this. He would drive through and pick up something to eat on the way in to the office.

"Hey, Mister! Hey, Mister!?"

Cameron awoke to the sound of a youngster's voice. Someone was sitting on his bed. Eyes still blurry from sleep, he looked up to find a toddler, a little boy, seated at his feet—or rather, on his feet.

"What in the world? . . ." Cameron mumbled sleepily. "What are you doing in here?"

"I two years old!" Zachary said, holding up four fingers.

"Great." Cameron pulled the covers up over his head. "Just great."

"Happy birthday to you! Happy birthday to you! Happy birthday, dear Cameron! Happy birthday to you!" His mother's happy smile loomed over him, cake blazing with four tiny candles.

A tender preschooler, he had clung to her skirt instead of blowing them out.

"I two years old!" Zachary shouted loudly, bringing him back. He jumped into Cameron's unsuspecting arms.

Great. Could things possibly get any better than this?

"I'm sorry," Shannon said, tapping on the young man's door. "That's my son you've got there."

She watched as he pulled the covers back, looking anything but friendly. If first impressions were telling, this one was a doozy.

"Come on, Zachary," she said hoarsely. "It's time for breakfast."

"Breakfast!" the toddler shouted at the top of his lungs. "Froot Loops!"

He jumped up and down on the bed, covers flying everywhere.

"Lady, could you get your kid off of me?" Cameron spoke angrily.

Quickly Shannon raced across the room, snatched Zachary and fled through the door. This was clearly one fella who did not want to be messed with.

Aaron Landers sat, gazing into the compassionate eyes of young Congressman Flannigan, content with the fact that he had found an ally.

"The sad part is, I think you and I both know where we're heading. We're in the process of eliminating ourselves as a human race," the congressman was saying.

"It's frightening," Aaron agreed. "That's why I felt I had no choice but to come and talk with you. After President Tinsdale's speech. . ."

"That was really something, wasn't it?"

"It's sad to see what we've become—a country bent on survival of the fittest," Aaron continued. "But at least she seems to be as concerned as we are. . . . That gave me some reason to hope."

"Me, too."

"Most legislators, yourself excluded of course, say they want to offer all human beings a 'humane right' to a dignified death." He could almost hear their words now. "The problem is, it's an impossible scenario—to think that we can provide this 'right' to some folks without denying it to others."

"It's the others that worry me," Flannigan said, shaking his head sadly. "The question they've never been able to answer is the one that bothers me most—How do we go about assessing the value of the life of a human being anyway?"

"It's pretty obvious they think that quality of life and sanctity of life are one and the same. I see a huge difference between the two!"

"The difference is," Congressman Flannigan interrupted, "that all of life has value. Most folks simply don't see that until it hits them close to home."

"Well, the way I look at it," Aaron added, "the day is coming, and soon, when it's going to hit every one of us a little too close to home."

"It's already happened in my family," Congressman Flannigan said, shaking his head. "I've got a niece just diagnosed with leukemia—my sister's daughter."

"I'm sorry," Aaron said gently.

Flannigan nodded. They were both sorry—about everything.

"Do you realize what's happening to the elderly?" Aaron added, almost whispering. "I don't mean the sick ones either. . . ."

"We call them autumn leaves," Flannigan said sadly. "Not quite time for them to drop to the ground, unless a strong wind comes along and blows them from the tree."

"Ouch."

"The argument is," the congressman continued, "they've already lived great lives, enjoyed good times, impacted society."

"And they have," Aaron argued. "But does that mean their contribution to society isn't worthwhile after a certain age? It seems to me that we have more to learn from the elderly than any group around. We have knowledge, but they have wisdom."

"I agree," Flannigan said, standing. "I've only been in office a few years, but I've been watching this downward spiral since I was a kid. I used to say that if parents were willing to pay money to eliminate their children, it would only be a matter of time before the children would be willing to pay money to eliminate their parents."

"I never thought about it from that angle," Aaron said, "but it makes sense. Our sins always seem to come back to haunt us, don't they?"

"Is that what you call this—sin?" Congressman Flannigan asked, looking at him intently.

Aaron felt his heart speed up a little. The last thing he wanted right now was an argument, but his emotions got the better of him.

"Yes, I call it sin," he said firmly. "What do you call it?"

A moment passed before the congressman gave his answer.

"It is sin. It's just so refreshing to hear someone state it so plainly. Most people wouldn't have the courage. In fact, most don't even acknowledge the fact that this is a spiritual problem. We're created in the image of God, but folks just don't see it— don't understand it."

Aaron bit his lip, debating how far he should go with this conversation. "Can I be really honest with you? . . ."

"Sure."

"Let's say. . .let's say I have a. . .friend."

"Go on."

"Let's say this friend is. . .terminal."

"Terminal?"

"Well, the diagnosis has been made. The truth is, this friend's got a better than fighting chance with a new medication, but this new law has tied her hands."

"Her? This is a woman?"

"Uh. . ." Aaron stammered. "I, uh. . ."

"Go on," Flannigan said with a smile. "My ears are open. My lips aren't."

"Well, let's say she's managed to avoid the inevitable—at least for the time being."

"Avoided it? How?"

Aaron felt his eyelids begin to twitch, a sure sign that he was nervous. "Let's just skip that part. . . . Anyway, let's say that she's still—out there—still free. Would it be possible to fight this thing in court?"

Congressman Flannigan seemed to stare a hole right through him, giving an intense answer. "It's already happening—all over the country. People are filing injunctions everywhere."

"How complicated is that?" Aaron asked. "And does it really accomplish anything, or just prolong the inevitable?"

"Well," Flannigan explained, "it's not so complicated, really. First your 'friend' would need to hire an attorney. He—I mean she—would then file an injunction in a United States court here in Houston, challenging the constitutionality of this law as it pertains to her right to 'life, liberty, and the pursuit of happiness.' "

"Go on. . . ," Aaron said, interested.

"From there the court in question would be required to review the law or pass the case on to a court of higher jurisdiction."

"Then what?"

"Then your friend spends time waiting—maybe a long time."

"But time. . .alive? Time without hiding, running? . . ."

"Sure," Flannigan assured him. "Once the injunction has been filed, the constitutionality of the law remains in question—often until the case hits the Supreme Court."

"Really?" There was hope!

"Really."

"So," Aaron asked hesitantly, "would this be the way to go? I mean, would you recommend this route?"

"Already have," Flannigan said with a smile. "We're filing with the local court here to keep my niece alive—at least until I can draft a bill to present to the House."

"You're working on it?" Aaron asked.

"Been working on it since the day the Duty law went into effect. The courts can't write or rewrite laws. Court rulings set a precedent for other cases, but everything is subject to interpretation by judges—judges who may be swayed by other forces, if you know what I mean. So it's up to legislators to do what they can."

"Oh, yeah."

"But this is happening every day. I just got another E-mail today from a family here in the area. Their baby, a Down's syndrome infant, has been moved to the Crossings nursery at Mercy. They've been told to just sit back and wait for his execution date."

"Can you help them?"

"I've got friends who can. In the meantime, I've got some of the best attorneys here in Houston and in D.C. working on a new bill," Flannigan said confidently. "Several other representatives in the House have already signed on, and others have said they'll back me all the way. It's not enough to fight this at the judicial branch. We've got to hit the legislative branch, too. We've already got the executive branch on our side."

"That's right. . . ."

"You and I aren't the only ones who are bothered by the law, you know," Flannigan continued. "It's hitting at the very core of what we stand for—our constitutional right to life. This is a law that was destined to fail even before it was implemented."

"What about Whitener?" Aaron asked, referring to a man who had made his reputation destroying lives.

"Whitener," Flannigan said, shuddering. "Thank God it's an election year. We can only hope the people in his district open their eyes and elect someone who cares about them. He and his friends are the instigators of this atrocity. Everyone on the Hill knows that. But his friends are fewer and fewer, thank God. It's just a matter of time."

"You really believe that?" Aaron asked, grinning.

"I sure do. It's just the folks that are already within their thirty-day waiting period that I'm really worried about—people like my niece—and your friend."

"Ashley," Aaron said, looking his congressman squarely in the eye.

"Ashley," Flannigan repeated with a smile.

Eighteen

So you're the Ashley I've heard so much about."

She looked up at Mason, smiling her response. He was a likable guy, at least from what she had casually observed, and seemed to be pretty easy to talk to. In fact, he seemed to be the one everyone went to when there was talking to be done.

"What have you heard?" she asked, genuinely wondering. Had Aaron said something?

"That you're a real fighter."

"Boy, that's the truth!" she said with a laugh. "I was born fighting."

"I meant fighting for your life. . . ."

"Oh. . ." Suddenly she felt more like hiding than fighting. He wasn't talking about her battles in the corporate world. He was talking about her life.

"It's a shame," Mason said sadly. "No one seems to have any respect for life anymore. It's amazing to think how far we've come just since I was your age."

"How old do you think I am?" she quizzed.

"Mmm. . . Twenty-three?"

"That's pretty conservative, I'd say. I'm twenty-seven. But I'll take that as a compliment." She laughed, in spite of herself. It felt really good.

"How are you holding up?" he asked, looking concerned.

"Pretty good, I guess," she said, eyes down. "But there's one thing I really miss. . . ."

"What's that?"

She couldn't hold back the grin as the words tumbled out. "Mint chocolate chip."

He laughed, long and loud. "Not quite what I was expecting you to say," he chided. "But. . .you may be in luck." He reached into the freezer, pulling out a half gallon of ice cream.

"You've got to be kidding me!" she said, amazed. "You mean, it's been there the whole time?"

"Yep. It's my favorite. Abbey always keeps it for me."

Well, if that didn't beat all! Maybe this place wouldn't be so bad after all.

Frank Carpenter dropped his briefcase down onto the chair in Paul Whitener's office, spilling its contents out all over the floor. "Great." It wasn't. Nothing was great these days, not since. . .

"Bad morning?" Paul Whitener asked, stepping inside.

"Uh, yeah," he mumbled, reaching down to scoop it up.

"What's going on?"

Frank knew better than to tell him the truth. With the kind of power that this particular congressman had, anything could happen to Shannon and the kids. Besides, no one had been any the wiser. Even Mildred, the woman who came to clean twice a week, thought that Shannon was away visiting relatives. So far, so good.

"Oh, I'm just a little tired, I guess," he said, forcing a yawn. "I was up late last night working on the paperwork for this bill."

That much was true. He had spent several hours through the night working on the wording of the Suicide Kit Bill, which the illustrious congressman would be introducing soon.

"Show me what you've got," Paul said, dropping into a chair.

"Well, I've done quite a bit of research since we spoke last," Frank said. "And I think I've implemented some wording that will fly."

"Wording is everything."

"I know. I know. And I've got a handle on the other thing. . . ."

"What other thing?"

"The issue of suicide for those who aren't ill."

"Tell me."

"Well, it would be sufficient to say that those who are contemplating suicide, particularly the healthy ones, are mentally ill. That would place them under the umbrella of government monies to purchase the kit. Getting the kit into their hands is the goal, right?"

"Yeah, right. But mentally ill?" Paul questioned. "I mean, just because someone is having a bad day and decides to do the unthinkable doesn't mean he's got a mental problem, does it?"

"You tell me." Frank felt his blood begin to boil. This guy was ready for an argument? Well, he would give him one. "Have you ever known anyone who was mentally ill, Paul? Do you have any idea the kinds of things they contemplate in the wee hours of the night?"

"There is some argument there, granted," Paul said with a shrug. "But listen, Frank, we've got to do better than that. All of us, at some crazy point, have thought about suicide. Someone hurts us—or we think our situation is hopeless—and bam, the word pops into our brain. It's just that most of us don't act on it."

"Because our mental state isn't warped," Frank argued. "See what I mean?"

He had never reached that point, in all honesty, but was certainly beginning to understand what pressure could do to one's mental state.

"There's more to it than that," Paul said. "And you know it. What these people need is hope."

"Hope? We're supposed to offer them hope?" Frank asked, throwing up his hands in frustration. "Excuse my stupidity, but doesn't that sort of defeat the purpose?"

"No way," Paul said with a smile. "We'll give them hope—packaged carefully in the form of an IV or needle."

Ah. It really was a matter of wording then.

"Pills aren't effective," Paul continued. "That much has been proven. So we'll have to move in the direction of something quicker and more potent."

"We'll need a new name then," Frank said, pondering the idea.

"Of course. I thought that was understood."

No longer angry, Frank's mind began to race through the possibilities. For some reason, the word "horizons" kept running through his mind. "What do you think of this?" he asked finally.

Paul turned to look at him. Frank amazed even himself with the next words. . ."Horizons of Hope."

There was a dead silence in the room for a moment. When Paul spoke, there was a trembling in his voice.

"My friend," he said, sticking out his hand, "I think you've got a winner."

Cameron was napping, lost in a dream. . . .

He was just a little thing, maybe six or seven, and his father was trying, rather impatiently, to teach him how to catch a softball.

"Hold your glove up like this," his dad was instructing.

He tried, diligently, but it was useless. The ball fell to the ground.

"Can't you do anything right?" His father's angry voice spoke volumes.

Cameron tossed and turned in the bed, his feet twisting the covers.

"Can't you do anything right?"

"Ouch!" He awoke quickly, Gilligan nipping at his toes. "Go away, dog!"

But the hyperactive puppy wasn't going away. He bounded up Cameron's legs, tongue lapping across his face as he landed, paws extended.

"Get out of here!" He tossed the puppy onto the floor just as Shannon appeared in the doorway.

"I'm sorry," she said, scooping Gilligan up. "I didn't know you were in here."

"Well, I am," he said angrily.

"Aren't you feeling well?"

"I'm just tired." Bored was more like it.

"Can we talk?" Shannon asked, looking a little worried.

Cameron shrugged. "I guess." He didn't really want to talk to her—didn't want anything to do with her, in fact.

She came in, sitting on the edge of the bed. "Is this okay?"

He shrugged again.

"Look," she said, "I feel like we need to declare a truce."

"What do you mean?"

"You don't like my kids, you don't like my dog, and you don't like me!" Shannon said, anger surfacing. "That's what I mean."

"I never said that," he argued. Forget the fact that she was right.

"Well, it's plenty obvious. And it's making me crazy," Shannon said. "I'm here because I have to be—just like you."

"You're not sick," he argued. "I don't even know why you're here."

"I'm pregnant."

"Big deal." They were cruel words, but the only ones that came to mind.

"They were going to make me give up the baby. You know. . . an abortion."

"What's wrong with that?" He didn't see the problem.

"I wouldn't expect you to understand," she argued. "But that's why I'm here. My reason is just as legitimate as yours."

"I didn't bring a whole city with me," he mumbled. He felt the guilt of the words before they even slipped out.

"I resent that."

"I'm sorry." He was, too. "Look, I'm just not used to kids. I've only got one brother, and he's twelve. He's really quiet. And no animals. None."

"Everyone needs someone to care about—and to care about him," Shannon said.

"I guess."

"Have you ever had that?"

It was an honest question. Only thing was, he didn't have an honest answer. Rolling over, he pulled the covers over his head.

"Could you shut the door on your way out?" he mumbled from under the sheets.

Jerome Patterson, P.I., pulled his '96 Explorer up to the emergency room entrance of Mercy Hospital. He pushed the door open, hopping out.

"Hey, you can't park there," an orderly out for a smoke said, pointing to the car.

Jerome shrugged, leaving the car and entering the door to the emergency room.

"I mean it," the orderly said angrily, tossing his cigarette. "They're gonna tow your car."

"Let them try," he mumbled. Moving toward the nurses' station, he pushed past waiting patients. "Where's the Crossings Unit?"

"You're on the wrong side of the hospital," the nurse said, barely looking up. "You've got to go down that hall, turn right at the first crossing. Take the elevator down to the tunnel system and follow the signs."

"You've got to be kidding me."

"Do I look like I'm kidding?" She looked up with a glare.

He shrugged, moving toward the hall. She wasn't worth wasting time over.

"Hey, fella," the orderly said, trailing him. "They're gonna. . ."

Jerome kept on moving, turning down the next hallway. Through a maze of elevators and tunnels he traveled, coming at last to the well-protected wing with the "Crossings" signs above.

At the nurses' station stood a frustrated-looking nurse, face worn with years, and perhaps worn with her duties, besides.

"Can I help you?" the middle-aged nurse asked abruptly.

He looked at her name tag before responding. Gina Evans. "Yes, Miss Evans. My name is Jerome Patterson. I need some information."

"What kind of information?" She looked a bit taken aback by his forwardness. That was fine. He motioned for her to speak privately. Maybe he'd better stoop to flirtatious tactics.

"Look, I'm pretty busy here," she tried to argue, turning the other way.

Fine. If that wouldn't work. . . "I'll make this worth your while," he said, pulling out two crisp hundred-dollar bills into her palm.

Her eyes grew large. "Who are you?" she whispered hoarsely.

"I'm. . . Let's just say I'm working for someone of importance here in the Houston area and in D.C., okay?"

She shrugged. "What do you want to know?"

Jerome was prepared for this. He pulled out a small notepad and a pen. "Tell me everything you know about underground intervention groups."

"What do you mean?" He couldn't help but notice the color draining from her cheeks.

"Oh, come on, Lady, you know what I mean. The intervention groups. They snatch your, uh. . .your 'patients' away when you're not looking."

"We're always looking," she said defiantly, shoving the money back in his hand. "And if you've come to accuse me of something, you can stop right there. This conversation is over."

Maybe this wasn't going to work. Time to slow things down. "Now, now. . .didn't mean to insult anyone." He pushed the money back toward her. "And I'm not here to hurt you. I'm here to help you."

"How?" There now. She was looking a little less nervous, and her grip on the bills had tightened somewhat.

"We're trying to get a handle on these groups—see how they're getting their people in, and how they're getting the patients out. Have you had any problems?"

"No."

"Ah, come on. Let's talk. I know you've lost a few along the way. I've made a few calls. . . ." He had. And there were missing bodies, whether she wanted to admit it or not.

"What kind of calls?"

"To the county authorities, for one thing. They have records of everyone who came through here. Problem is, there were no funeral services for many of them. . . ."

"That's easy enough to explain. Half these 'patients' don't opt for funerals. Their bodies are donated to the medical center for scientific research—after organ donation, of course."

"The ones who actually go through the process, you mean."

"I don't get your meaning."

Sure she did. "Look, Sister—I just have a list of names here. . . . I'd like to check it against your records."

Now she was mad. "Our records are confidential. I can't let anyone see them without a court order. I don't care who you're working for."

"That's easy enough to get," he said smoothly. "But why don't you make things easy on me?" He slipped another bill into her hand.

"You'll have to do better than that."

Just as he suspected. "You're a persistent one!" Another two hundreds fell into her waiting palm.

"Meet me in the records room in exactly twenty minutes," she mumbled, looking around.

"Where's that?"

She signaled to a door about halfway up the hall.

With a nod, he turned in the opposite direction.

Nurse Gina Evans's heart was beating so hard, she could scarcely breathe. Who was this guy, and what did he want with her? Was he really with the government? If so, she might be doing herself a favor giving him the records. If not. . . Well, if not, it could very well be the end of her nursing days. Of course, this wasn't the first time she had risked her career for a handful of bills. . . . That much was true.

She slipped into a patient's room, acting casual.

"Everything okay in here?" she asked.

The nurse in charge nodded. "Sure."

In the bed an elderly woman with Alzheimer's was slowly drifting from this world to another.

"Just the usual," the nurse said with a yawn. "Why? What's up?"

"Nothing. Just doing my job." Gina turned from the room, the door clicking firmly shut behind her.

The next twenty minutes seemed more like hours. She reached the records room just one step ahead of the stranger who called himself Mark Johnson. Once inside, they stood side by side in the records room, poised and ready, like friends on the same team.

"What about this one?" he asked, quickly pointing to his list.

"Billy Pfeiffer? Let's see. . . ," she whispered, fumbling through the files. "Oh, here it is. His body was donated."

"Hmm. This one?" He pointed to a name. For some reason, it almost seemed to jump off the page at her.

"Ashley Cooper?" She remembered Ashley like it was yesterday. That nice young doctor had. . .

"Any information on her?"

She thumbed through the files, eyes huge. "No. Why?"

"No burial record from the county, that's all."

"Well, she's more than dead, I can assure you. I was there myself."

"Were you now?"

"Yes. I. . .I. . ."

Gina had never been very good at lying, even as a child. It looked like the game was suddenly, but finally, up.

"What's going on in here?" Blaine Bishop swung the door of the records room open wide. "What are you doing?"

Something was definitely up, though Blaine couldn't be sure if he was rescuing Nurse Gina Evans or catching her in the act. Her eyes were wide with fear, either way. One thing was for sure, the pimply-faced guy with the slicked-back hair certainly didn't belong in here.

"Jerome Patterson," the fellow said, sticking out his hand. "And you would be. . ."

"The one in charge," came his swift reply. "Blaine Bishop."

"Ah ha. . .a name I know as well as my own."

"You know me?" That intrigued him, though curiosity was shaded with serious distrust.

"You bet. Sure I know you. You're the infamous Dr. Bishop. Head of 'Crossings.' "

"What does that have to do with you?" Blaine repeated, trying to look more assured than he felt. "And what are you doing in here?"

"Well, Dr. Bishop," Jerome said bluntly. "It looks like you have a little problem on your hands. I might just have to do something about it."

Blaine pushed the door shut behind him, feeling his heart begin to race.

Do something!

"What. . .what do you mean?" he stammered.

"Missing bodies, live people who should be dead, intrigue, mystery—all the makings of a TV movie."

"What are you talking about?"

"Ashley Cooper," Jerome said, looking him in the eye. "Looks like we've got a live wire."

Blaine suddenly felt sick.

Nineteen

Ashley padded across the kitchen in her bare feet. Havensbrook was a homey place. To be honest, she had really learned to enjoy her days in this spot, nestled in the pines. Unlike life in the city, things were quiet here, almost peaceful. Instead of dirty gray, this place actually had color—lots of it. The old wooden house was fashioned after the East Texas log-cabin style of days gone by. It was large and roomy. The pines were alive with color and fragrance, and roses bloomed in Abbey's garden just outside the back door.

Abbey. She was nothing short of wonderful, and Mason was quickly becoming a father figure to Ashley. There were those times, when everything was dark and quiet, that Ashley found herself missing her mother with an ache almost as severe as that induced by death, but those times were fewer and farther between. In those fragile moments, she found herself caught up with memories of her father, and dreams of yellow roses often followed.

Ashley even felt herself missing Aaron, as well. She almost looked forward to starting treatment in a few days, just so she could see him again.

"How do you like your coffee?" Abbey asked, as Ashley sat at the table.

"Oh, here," she said, rising. "Let me get that. I'm no invalid." It was awkward to be waited on, especially by someone as giving as Abbey.

"You're a guest in my home," Abbey responded. "And I don't mind."

"Well, one sugar then—and a little cream."

Three or four of the others came in, interrupting their conversation. Ashley didn't mind. She was almost learning to enjoy the chaos.

"Is the paper here?" old Joe Reynolds asked.

He was a stickler for checking the weather report every day, though he rarely had the ability to spend much time out of doors.

"In the living room, Joe," Abbey responded, "on the sofa."

He turned to leave the room, old Mitsy Jansen following him out. Alzheimer's had already left its ugly stain on her life, but she had found a friend in Joe Reynolds.

"Living room, Joe. Living room, Joe," she echoed numbly.

"Old woman, if you don't stop following me! . . ." he mumbled.

Ashley couldn't help but laugh.

"He's a hoot," Abbey said, handing her the cup of coffee. "I think he secretly has a crush on her."

Crush. Just the word made Ashley think of Aaron, though she didn't know why.

"What's for lunch, Abbey?" Deena Marie asked, interrupting her thoughts. The youngest of the "patients" at Havensbrook, Deena was only thirteen. Sickle cell anemia was a daily struggle.

"We're having that homemade chicken and dumplings you love so much," Abbey said. "Now shoo, Girl! I need to spend a little time with Ashley."

With a pout, Deena left the room.

"I don't need any special treatment," Ashley said, feeling guilty. After all, Abbey had a whole household to run, many guests to tend to. She was no one special.

"In God's eyes, we're all special," her hostess answered.

There she went with that God thing again. It was the only problem with this place.

"What God?" Ashley mumbled. She looked down at the floor, unable to catch what she was sure would be a glare from

Abbey. When she did look up, all she saw was tenderness.

"The one who spared your life," the older woman said. "The one who brought you here to us."

"I don't really believe in God," Ashley answered, choosing her words carefully. "I guess you could say I believe in. . .in. . .the human spirit. You know. . .the power of the individual." There. That should be satisfactory.

"So you rescued yourself then?" Abbey asked gently. "Is that what you're saying?"

Ouch. That hurt.

"I'm just saying," Ashley explained almost stubbornly, "that if there were a God, then I wouldn't be in this mess in the first place."

"Really?"

"How could a loving God—"

"—let something like this happen to me?" Abbey finished the sentence with her. . . .

Ashley stared hard at her, feeling tears well up.

"The eternal question! And a question I've heard more than a few times around here, if you don't mind my saying," Abbey added, grinning. "The answer I always give is this: 'God's heart is broken over what has happened to you.' "

"But He could have stopped it." Ashley's heart twisted inside her. "I mean. . .if He existed. . ."

"We live in a fallen world, Honey. All sorts of things happen because of the sin of mankind."

"Are you saying I got sick because I'm a sinner?" Ashley's blood began to boil.

"Definitely not. Definitely not!"

"Then what?"

"This is no Garden of Eden we're living in—and for that reason alone there are going to be hardships in our lives."

Ashley shrugged. "I just don't get it. Why would God rescue me, only to have me die all over again?"

"We're all going to die sooner or later, Ashley. There's a time to be born and a time to die. It just wasn't your time yet, that's all."

"But. . ."

"I don't have all the answers," Abbey said plainly. "But I know someone who does."

"That's such a cop-out," Ashley argued, feeling the anger swell. "And it's not like I don't know anything about God. I heard about Him the whole time I was growing up—not that I cared to."

"You did?" Abbey's face expressed her concern. "What were you told?"

Oh, the things that she had been told! There weren't enough hours in the day to repeat them—not in this setting. How could she explain?

"I had an aunt who was a Christian," Ashley said, feeling her ears begin to pulsate. "She was the cruelest woman I ever met. I couldn't do anything right in her eyes. No one could."

That was an understatement. Aunt Sharon had told her dozens of times that she was going to hell. There was nothing she could do to change that. Trembling began with the memories.

"I didn't know her," Abbey responded, "so I can't really say—but maybe she had some issues in her life that you weren't aware of."

"There were issues all right." The words slipped out, laced with bitterness.

"Honey, I think you'll find that most Christians are good, loving people."

Ashley took a deep breath, trying to calm herself. What was it that still got her so angry when Aunt Sharon came up? It was over, done. The woman had died a miserable death, alone and angry. She had gotten what she deserved in the end.

Looking up, Ashley caught Abbey's eye.

"You know, Honey," the older woman said, "unforgiveness is like a cancer. It can take root in your life and grow so big that it finally consumes you. In some ways, it's worse than a physical cancer."

That made no sense at all. "I'm supposed to forgive someone who hurt me and never even took the time to apologize?" The anger began to rise to the surface again.

"Forgiveness is like a key," Abbey explained gently. "It unlocks the prison doors."

"Prison?" This conversation had definitely taken a wrong turn.

"When you hold someone in unforgiveness," Abbey continued, "it's like holding them in a prison. Worse still, the real prison is the one you place yourself in when you choose not to forgive. It takes a great deal of time and effort to hold a grudge."

That was true, but. . .

"There is forgiveness," Abbey continued, "but it comes with a pretty hefty price tag attached. . . ."

"Everything in church has a price tag attached," Ashley mumbled, feeling her eyes shift to the floor.

"No, you don't understand," Abbey said gently. "This is a price that you could never afford to pay—even if you worked every day for the rest of your life. That's why God sent His Son to the cross."

There was apparently no turning back now. Ashley began to squirm uncomfortably.

"When Jesus died on the cross," Abbey explained, "it was the ultimate act of forgiveness. It cost God everything."

"Why? I mean, let's say this whole God thing is real. That still doesn't explain why He would do something like that. He didn't have to do that." It didn't make any sense. It wasn't logical.

"That's right," Abbey said, nodding. "He didn't have to. He chose to."

"That sounds too easy—like a fairy tale or something," Ashley said. "What's the catch?" She felt uneasy with the question, but still she knew that there would be a catch. There was always a catch. "I mean, what's it going to cost me?"

"Ah," Abbey said with a smile. "That's easy. The cost lies in the choosing."

A mysterious answer. Ashley shrugged again. "The choosing?"

"Yes, the choosing. 'Choose you this day whom you will serve. As for me and my house, we will serve the Lord.' "

Well, that certainly explained a lot.

"What about Aaron?" Ashley asked hesitantly. "Does he. . .I mean, is this what he believes, too?"

"Oh, Aaron," the older woman said with a smile. "He believes all right. In fact, he believes so strongly that he risks his life every day to step into the fire and pull people out. He's given up everything—a good job, his safety—all to help others."

Ashley suddenly felt a searing of guilt. He had snatched her from the fire. She should be grateful. She should be—

"You've got to understand, Ashley," Abbey continued. "Aaron has lost a lot in his life. An awful lot. Like all of us, he's had to forgive both others. . .and himself."

"Are you talking about what happened to his parents?" Now they were getting somewhere.

"Yes, and so much more," Abbey explained. "Did you know that for years Shannon wouldn't speak to him?"

"Why?" This certainly aroused her curiosity.

"I think she secretly blamed him for the death of their parents."

"What do you mean?"

"He wasn't responsible," Abbey said, patting her on the hand, "but in Shannon's eyes, he should have been there to prevent it."

"Man. And I thought I had lost a lot," Ashley mumbled. She had, after all, lost her apartment, her car, her fashionable clothing.

"I guess the question is: What are things," Abbey asked gently, "when you have your life? 'What does it profit a man to gain the whole world? . . .' "

Ashley was stunned by her next words. . .

"Only to lose his soul?"

"How long have you known?"

Cameron looked up from his living room chair to find June Ann, the only other HIV-positive person at Havensbrook. For nearly a week he had been avoiding her. . .like the plague, in fact.

"What's it to you?" he asked, flipping the pages of a novel as if he were reading.

"I've known for three years," she said. "Since I was twenty-two."

He shrugged. "I just found out a few months ago."

"You're not sick, then?"

"No. Not that it's any of your business. And I'm not going to get sick." He slammed the book down on the end table, disrupting a conversation between old Joe Reynolds and Mitsy Jansen across the room.

Now June Ann shrugged. "I just started showing symptoms about the time, well, you know. . ."

"What do you mean?"

"About the time of the. . .the law."

"Oh, sorry." He was sorry. Sorry for both of them. No, sorry for all of them. His heart, already softened, suddenly began to melt.

"Look," he said softly. "I'm sorry. I got off to a bad start this morning. Could we start over again?"

"Sure," she said with a grin. "Hi. My name is June Ann, and I'm HIV-positive."

"My name is Cameron," he said, sticking out his hand. "And I. . .well, I am, too." It was difficult to say, but somehow saying it almost brought a sense of relief. The truth was out.

The two began a conversation as if they were old friends. June Ann shared her story, telling about a life of drugs with an HIV-positive payoff. When it came time for Cameron to speak, he hardly knew where to begin.

"I, uh, I was just diagnosed a little while ago, like I said," he spoke, not looking up. "I was, uh. . ." How could he say it? "I've been involved in an 'alternative lifestyle' since I was about twelve."

"Oh." She didn't look terribly shocked.

"When I was diagnosed, I had to tell my family." This memory was as clear as water. It had been the hardest thing he had ever done. "My mom was. . .well, it really tore her up—but she loved me, you know?"

June Ann nodded, obviously understanding.

"But my dad," he continued. "That was a lot tougher. My dad

was never really around much when I was growing up. I think I always wanted his attention from the time I was just a kid. And now I had it. But this wasn't the kind of attention I wanted, and. . ." He felt the familiar lump in his throat, remembering.

"Go ahead. It's okay."

"He, uh, he told me. . ."

"You're dead! You hear that, Cameron? You're dead to me!"

Cameron felt a tear slip down his cheek but didn't care. "He said that as far as he was concerned, I was already dead. Then he just turned and walked out of the room. That was the last time I ever saw him."

"I'm sorry," June Ann whispered, reaching for his hand.

Cameron spoke over the lump that was growing in his throat. "After that I headed out to the streets to avoid being picked up. I found a spot in downtown Houston. . .an abandoned building, to be honest."

"And?"

"There were a few of us there. We did what we could to survive."

She understood. It was clear by the look on her face. He had sold himself to the highest bidder, given himself over to a lower class of people. There was no denying it.

"I. . .I. . ."

"Go on," she said, squeezing his hand. "I can take it."

"I, uh, I heard about this guy who used to come and hang out on the street corners and bring food. He was from some local church or something, I don't really know. Anyway, one of the guys told me that he could help me."

"Help bring you here?"

"Anywhere," Cameron said. "I would have been willing to go anywhere but where I was."

"So he brought you here?"

"No. I started off at another safe house, but they were about to be raided, so I ran. One of the guys there told me about a place he had heard of called Havensbrook. . .told me where he thought it was and mumbled something that sounded like a password."

It had all happened so quickly, so mysteriously.

"But how did you get here?" June Ann looked worried.

"I ran."

"Cameron, tell the truth."

He was. Every word was true.

"I started late at night from downtown Houston. I only moved at night when I was in the city, but once I got to the outskirts of town, I knew I could only make it through the forest in daylight."

"You came all that way on foot?" She looked amazed.

"Yes." He pulled up his pants legs, showing her the jagged cut marks where the underbrush of the forest had eaten away at him as he ran.

"That's a miracle, Cameron," she said, eyes growing large. "Do you know what a miracle that is?"

Miracle? Cameron shrugged, suddenly ready for the conversation to end. There was nothing miraculous about his situation.

Shannon entered the living room, toddler on one hip and Veronica clinging to her right hand.

"How're ya gonna hold the next one?" Joe Reynolds asked.

It was a good question. She was already out of hands. Once this baby was born. . . No. She wouldn't think about that.

"I want to go outside and play, Mommy!" Zachary cried, interrupting her thoughts.

"You can't go out right now, Honey!" she answered angrily.

How could she explain to a two year old that he might be endangering the lives of this many people by creating too much noise outside?

"Can I have a cookie?" he asked, pouting.

"Ask Abbey," she answered, putting him down.

He toddled off toward the kitchen. Shannon looked across the room. In the wing chair sat Cameron, the young man who had taken such a liking to her son. He was visiting quietly with June

Ann, a young woman who had remained mysterious and somewhat aloof. Shannon opted to move toward the den in the back of the house.

"I'm bored, Mom," Veronica said. "There is nothing to do here."

"Uncle Aaron is getting some schoolbooks for you," Shannon said firmly. "And then you'll have plenty to do."

"Can't we just go home?" she whined. "I miss my friends. And I miss Daddy, too."

"Honey, I told you. . ."

Shannon didn't even finish the conversation. There was nothing she could say that hadn't already been spoken. Someday her children would understand that what she was doing was noble, valiant. . . .

Veronica rolled her eyes dramatically as they entered the den. Shannon looked around the room. It, too, was full of people.

"Hi, Shannon!" It was Mary Lewis. They had met at breakfast. Mary had multiple sclerosis and had been with Mason and Abbey the longest of anyone here.

"Hey," was all she could answer.

"Mom, can I watch TV?" Veronica said.

"Do you mind?" Shannon asked, looking around the room.

They shrugged, turning their attention back to conversation.

"They don't even have cable," Veronica mumbled, grabbing the remote.

Shannon shook her head, half apologetically to the others in the room.

"You're the ones with the dog, right?" Deena Marie asked, turning toward Veronica.

"Yeah! He's Gilligan."

"Where's he at?"

"In the backyard, I think," Shannon answered for her daughter.

"Can we play with him?"

Veronica looked up at her mother, eyes pleading, thrilled to have made a new friend. "Please, Mom."

"If Abbey says it's okay, the two of you can take him into the barn and play in there."

The two girls jumped up, heading off toward the kitchen, nearly knocking over Zachary, who entered the den, cookie crumbs everywhere.

"Look, Mommy!" he shouted. "Cookie!"

"Zachary!"

"It's okay, Shannon," Mason said, entering the room. "He can make all the mess he wants. We don't mind."

Shannon stared up into the eyes of this man, the one who had loved and cared for her, even as a child—the only Sunday school teacher she had ever really tolerated.

"You know," Mason said, looking at Mary, "I used to teach Shannon when she was a little girl."

"You did?" Mary asked, obviously curious.

"Yep. She was in the. . ."

"Fifth grade," Shannon reminded him, smiling.

"Fifth grade," he echoed. "And man, oh man, was she ever a handful."

"Huh! What's that supposed to mean?"

But she knew what he meant. Shannon had never really fit in at church, even as a child. She had always felt inadequate, always felt as if nothing she did was good enough. She couldn't please her mother, her father. . .

Stop it! she said to herself abruptly. How could she think about them like that?

"She was the best student I ever had," Mason said, looking at her tenderly.

His words took Shannon's breath away.

"Really?"

"Really," he said, smiling. "You were a smart little whipper-snapper and didn't always have to be the center of attention."

"Like Aaron, you mean?"

"Well, you have to admit, he was always right there. . . ."

155

"Except when we needed him to be," Shannon mumbled.

"What do you mean?" Mason asked carefully.

Shannon's heart began to pick up. Part of her wanted to spill her emotions out in the telling of the story. Another part of her wanted to lock it safely away in the closet that had held it captive for three long years.

Three years. Had it really been three years? She suddenly realized how desperately she needed to talk to someone.

TWENTY

The Oval Office was all abuzz.

"Madame President," Charlotte's secretary beeped in, "you've got a call on line three. It's Prime Minister Henley."

Charlotte should be used to this by now, but she wasn't. The inconveniences were piling up, and everything was beginning to run together. There were bills to veto, campaign fund-raisers to go thank, dinners to give, legislation to encourage. It had all spilled over onto itself, creating a mess in her mind.

Which was which? Was she supposed to veto the current spending bill or not? Was the issue of education still needing to be addressed, or had she already taken care of that? Was the gun control package in the House or the Senate? Would she veto it when it reached her desk or not?

No. Right now the prime minister was on line three.

She took the call, anxious to get back to the work at hand. There was a stack of paperwork on her desk, days' worth of items needing signatures, responses. There was also a stack of letters, congratulations mostly, from her friends and constituents back in Montana.

Finishing the conversation, she placed the phone back on the hook. Charlotte took a deep breath, reaching down to pick up a letter with a familiar letterhead.

"Dear Charlotte," the letter read. *Ah! Someone still remembers my name!* "We miss you at the PTA meetings. Billings will never be the same without you!" It was signed by Jonathan's sixth-grade teacher back home.

Charlotte smiled, remembering. The smile melted quickly as she reached for the next letter.

"Madame President," this one read, "I'm looking forward to working with you. It is my hope that we can find a common meeting ground on the Duty to Die issue."

Hmm.

It was signed by her favorite foe—Congressman Paul Whitener. Just thinking about him sent a chill up her spine. He was everything a politician shouldn't be—at least to her way of thinking.

Charlotte looked up suddenly, hearing the rap on the door.

"Madame President?" It was the doctor who had come to examine Jonathan. "Could I speak with you?"

"Yes, please. . . ," she said, standing. "I could use a break."

The elderly man entered, his face somewhat expressionless.

"So what's the verdict?" Charlotte asked with a smile. "Just playing hooky?"

His lack of an immediate answer caused her insides to churn with fear.

"I don't think so," he said, taking a seat. "In fact, Madame President, I think we need to talk."

Numbly, she dropped into the chair.

Coral dialed the number for the umpteenth time, content in the fact that she had finally found an ally. This was a miracle—nothing more, nothing less. And a miracle was exactly what they had been needing.

"What's the plan?" she asked hesitantly, clutching the phone in her right hand.

"We meet on the steps of the courthouse in an hour," Congressman Flannigan said breathlessly. "Just be prepared to do battle."

Prepared? She was more than prepared.

Ashley dropped onto the sofa, completely relaxed. She let her eyes close momentarily. It felt wonderful.

"How are you?" She looked up to see Shannon standing next to her, eyes strangely misty.

"What do you mean?"

"You know," Shannon said, sitting. "Physically. How are you doing?"

To be honest, it was the first time in days that Ashley had been reminded of her illness. Once a looming shadow, it now seemed more like a distant memory.

"I'm feeling pretty good, all things considered," she answered.

"Not sick?"

"No," Ashley said, realizing the depth of those words. "It's the strangest thing. I've been feeling good, really good. Abbey started me on some kind of enzymes and some herbs—I don't really know what all they are—but I've never felt better."

"That's great."

What about you? Ashley wanted to ask the question but didn't dare. It was obvious Shannon was dealing with something, and she didn't want to seem nosy.

"Mama, I'm sleepy!" Zachary interrupted their conversation, pulling on Shannon's skirt.

"Come here, Babe," she said, pulling him up into her lap.

Though she didn't know why, Ashley felt a strange twinge of jealousy while watching the two of them. Would she ever have children? Would she ever have a loving husband?

"I'm glad to hear you're doing well," Shannon said, interrupting her thoughts. "I've been praying for you."

"Praying?" There it was again—the religion thing.

"Well, just this afternoon, really," Shannon said, her eyes looking misty again. "After talking to Mason."

Ah. A way to change the subject.

"Speaking of Mason," Ashley interjected. "I think he called your brother last night."

"I was wondering how he was doing."

"Busy. At least that's what Mason and Abbey said."

"Yeah, I think he's always on the go," Shannon responded. "At least he used to be. To be perfectly honest, I really don't know my brother very well. We've grown apart over the last few years."

Ah. Another door opened.

"I, uh," Ashley stumbled over her words. "I've been trying to work up the courage to ask you about that. I mean. . .I couldn't help but notice some strain there."

"It's pretty complicated," Shannon said, eyes dropping. "It goes back to when my parents were killed."

Another question answered.

"You don't have to tell me if it's too hard," Ashley said, taking her hand. "It's really none of my business."

"To be honest," Shannon said, a tear working its way down her cheek, "I've never talked to anyone about it until today—not even Frank."

"Frank's your husband, right?"

Shannon's face contorted slightly. It would have been impossible not to notice. "Yes," she said, barely whispering.

"What's he like? Like Aaron?"

Shannon's expression changed dramatically, a smile curling up at the edge of her lips. "No. No way. They're polar opposites."

"What do you mean?"

"Aaron is really. . .soft, caring. . ." Shannon explained. "He could never turn away a stray—you know what I mean?"

Ashley couldn't help but smile. "Yeah," she answered. "That's pretty clear."

Shannon, apparently lost in her thoughts, continued on. "But Frank. . .well, Frank is another story. He's really hard."

Another tear.

"I'm sorry," Ashley said, giving her hand a squeeze.

"No," came Shannon's swift reply. "I'm the one who's sorry. Sorry about a lot of things. But I feel a little better about everything now that I've talked to Mason. Did you know he was my

Sunday school teacher when I was a kid?"

"I heard that," Ashley said, "but I still can't imagine your brother sitting still through a Sunday school class."

"Who said anything about sitting still?" Shannon asked, smiling. "He was a brat when he was a kid. But he's still in Sunday school. Bet you didn't know that."

"What?" Ashley couldn't believe her ears.

"Yeah. In fact," Shannon added, "I think he actually teaches a Sunday school class at some little church not far from his apartment."

Ashley felt a twinge of disappointment shoot through her. This guy was definitely not for her. Enough said.

"I haven't been to church since my parents died," Shannon said, shrugging. "It was too hard. I just couldn't go back. I had too many questions."

"I understand that," Ashley said with a smirk. "I've never had anything but questions. . .at least as far as God is concerned. And people like your brother have never had anything but answers."

"Is that so bad?" Shannon asked, looking her in the eye.

"No," Ashley said, shifting her focus. "As long as they're the right answers."

"I'm sure that even Aaron makes mistakes," Shannon said. "But he's a really good guy. It took a conversation with Mason to see just how good."

"You blamed Aaron for your parents' death?"

There. She had spoken the dreaded question.

"I did," Shannon said, the tears now coming in pairs. "But not anymore."

"It's been quite a day," Mason said, letting himself relax on the porch swing.

Abbey responded with two quiet words, apparently all that she could muster: "I'm beat."

She looked beat, though he would never have said that. Abbey had worked particularly hard today. June Ann wasn't feeling well, and some of the elderly guests had needed extra attention.

"Need a back rub?" Mason asked, standing.

"If you're offering. . ."

He stepped behind the swing, placing his hands on her shoulders. They gave way to his touch, aching for attention. He began to rub with a vigor. She deserved it. She deserved so much more, in fact.

"That was a great dinner, Abbey. I don't know how you do it."

He didn't. And yet she always seemed to be able to keep up with—even keep ahead of—the game.

"You can thank Aaron for that," she said, pushing back up the bifocals that had slipped precariously down her nose. "He had a truckload of vegetables and meats brought up this morning when you were down at the clinic."

Clinic. They could barely call it that. It was just a little building up the road a bit used to store medical supplies for their guests. Aaron used it on occasion when the need arose. Thank God they hadn't needed it much.

"Anyone we know?" Mason asked, a little nervous, directing his attention back to the driver. Even though Havensbrook was off the beaten path, it was still dangerous to have people coming and going. He was keenly aware of this.

"No. This was a new kid. But Aaron warned me ahead of time. He said not to worry. I didn't."

She never did. She was the most trusting person he had ever known.

"Well, anyway, that was a great ham—and those potatoes were straight from heaven."

"I notice you ate a plateful," she said with a smile. "What happened to that low-carb diet you were going to go on?"

Mason rubbed his extended belly, grinning. "I am on a diet," he said with a smirk. "A seafood diet. I see food. . ."

". . .and you eat it." She finished the sentence for him. It wasn't the first time, and it certainly wouldn't be the last.

"Okay to come out?" Shannon spoke the words hesitantly, stepping out onto the porch. Mason and Abbey were enjoying some time together, probably pretty rare these days.

"Sure, Hon," Abbey said. "I don't think you need to stay cooped up inside all the time. We're pretty far off the beaten path, and besides. . .it's late."

Shannon stepped out, letting the evening breeze envelop her. It was delicious. She breathed it in, momentarily forgetting why she was here, what she was doing. . . .

"Shannon?" Mason's voice nudged her back.

"Yes?"

"I just wanted to thank you for the conversation this afternoon. I really enjoyed it."

No. She was the one who had enjoyed it. He was the one. . . Well, he was the one who had forced her to look at her relationship with her brother through God's eyes. He was the one who had convinced her that forgiveness was not only the best thing for Aaron, it was the best thing for her, as well.

"You're easy to talk to," she said, looking the older man in the eye. "It's been a long time since I've had a dad."

"Well, you've got one now," Mason said, standing. He reached over, thrusting his burly arms around her neck, swallowing her up in a fatherly embrace. Shannon felt the tears begin to slip down her cheeks, slowly at first, then rushing like a current. Her chest heaved in and out with the sobs that came almost naturally. This man wasn't her father. Her father was. . .

But surely this man and this woman had been sent to her at just the right time. That was undeniable.

"Congressman Flannigan! Congressman Flannigan!" The reporters vied for his attention.

Mike Flannigan cleared his throat, preparing to speak to the crowd. This press conference was being held at his bidding, and he was more than prepared for them. At his side stood Coral and Jacob Summerlin, here by invitation, prepared to tell their story to a waiting public. Getting the story out to the people was his best bet.

"Are we ready?" he asked.

A nod from nearby cameramen was his go-ahead.

"Ladies and gentlemen, I've called this press conference today," he began, eyes straight ahead, "because I have growing concerns about the implications of the Duty to Die law. From its inception, it has been a cancer of sorts, spreading much like the disease itself. But how did we get to this point? That's the question I'd like to ask. . .not the lawmakers—but you, the voting public."

He plowed ahead. "You know, back in the early 1990s there was a great deal of concern over doctor-assisted suicide from those in the medical community. That was when they still had a voice, of course. At that time, most agreed that a doctor did not hold the right to act with the intent to cause death. I have always felt that the job of medical practitioners should be to save lives, not take them. Those in the medical community used to share my beliefs. But at some point, things began to turn."

Boy, had they ever.

"Now here we are—facing a sea of death, and wondering how we got here. And yet it all seems so antiseptic, so impersonal—until it hits you."

Here he paused, looking at Coral and Jacob. They looked nervous, tense. Would they be able to go through with this?

"That is why I have invited my new friends, Coral and Jacob Summerlin," he said, nodding in their direction, "to speak with you."

Coral felt her heart begin to race. She had always been a little shy in front of people. In fact, she couldn't even get through a speech in drama class as a teen. What in the world was she doing, standing before a crowd of this size, speaking to people across the country? She was doing it for her son.

"Hello. . . ," she said hesitantly. She felt Jacob's strong hand on her shoulder. It gave her the courage to continue on. "Hello, I'm Coral Summerlin, and this is my husband, Jacob."

Feeling her hands begin to shake, she gripped the picture in her hand all the tighter. "I'm here today," she said, "because I want to tell you about our son, Jamie."

She lifted the picture of the baby for the crowd to see. Townspeople had gathered on the streets, many just nosy—some wanting to get their faces on the news. It didn't matter. Right now they were her allies.

Jamie had been in the incubator when the picture had been taken. In fact, Coral had slipped into the nursery during off-hours to take it when no one was watching.

Oohs and aahs went up from the crowd as the camera zoomed in on the infant's tiny face.

"Jamie is just ten days old," she explained, holding the picture before the cameras. "And we've been told that he only has twenty more days to live."

The gasp that went up from the crowd gave her the courage to go on.

"Jamie isn't going to die of natural causes," she said angrily. "The doctors at Houston's Mercy Hospital are going to kill him in twenty days."

A low rumble began among the crowd.

"Jamie is one of many children in the United States born with Down's syndrome," Coral explained, "a chromosomal abnormality. The Duty to Die law has tied the hands of parents everywhere. Our children are dying, and no one cares."

Another rumble. There were those in the crowd who obviously cared.

"I don't want my son to die," Coral spoke passionately. "My husband and I are going to do whatever it takes to save his life. We want you to join with us."

At this, Congressman Flannigan stepped next to her. "This new law is a blight, and we must stop it before things go any further. We're urging you to write your legislators and let them know how you feel. No doubt many of your lives—or the lives of your loved ones—have already been affected."

Coral felt the impact of his words.

"What about the baby?" a reporter cried out. "What are you doing to save him?"

A knot rose up in her throat, and she knew that tears were inevitable. The congressman answered, much to her relief.

"The Summerlins' attorney, Joe Harris, of Harris, Blodgett, and Claire, has just filed for an injunction this morning."

"What's that mean?" a reporter quizzed, writing frantically.

Coral and Jacob had only just learned what it meant this very morning. It was risky, and a bond would have to be posted, but it was the only chance they had.

"It means," Flannigan explained, "that we can probably prevent, or at the very least, prolong, little Jamie's unnatural death. A case will be brought before a judge, here in Harris County. He or she can then instruct the violator—in this case, Mercy Hospital—not to act in violation of Baby Jamie's rights, as protected under the Constitution of the United States."

"Will they have to let the baby go?" the reporter asked, still scribbling.

"That decision will have to be by the judge," Flannigan spoke again. "But we are hopeful, since the baby has no medical reason to remain hospitalized, that he will be released to the parents soon. Of course, we're really looking at a permanent injunction. Once the judge makes a final ruling, Jamie may be free to live a long, healthy life."

Those were the words Coral clung to. She held the picture back up. "We would like to ask all of you to pray for our son. Pray for his life. Pray for his safety. Like so many others, he hasn't done anything wrong. He deserves a chance for life, liberty, and the pursuit of happiness—just like everyone else."

Her knees buckled, and she felt a little faint. The crowd began to sway. . .or was it the crowd?

"That concludes this press conference," she heard Flannigan say.

"Mrs. Summerlin! Mr. Summerlin!" the reporters called out

madly, pulling at them from every conceivable direction.

Coral turned one direction and then another, firing rapid responses to anxious questions. Everything after that became a blur.

Aaron Landers stood off to the side, watching the press conference with great interest. From here, he and Congressman Flannigan would convene at Attorney Joe Harris's office, where they would be filing a similar injunction on Ashley Cooper's behalf.

He was completely unaware of the cameraman from Channel 13 scoping the crowd. In fact, Aaron had no way of knowing the effect his presence here would have on the underground movement.

"You need to watch this."

Nurse Gina Evans spoke nervously. Blaine Bishop turned to face her.

"What?" he asked, glancing down at the television in the Crossings lounge.

"It is a press conference. They are talking about us," she explained.

"Us? What do you mean?"

Blaine had been a nervous wreck for the last couple of days, ever since Jerome Patterson's unexpected visit. But things seemed to have settled down in the Crossings wing, Gina observed. If only she could keep it that way.

"Just listen."

They watched the press conference in relative silence. "Please. . ." and "Oh, Brother" were the only words either spoke, words occasionally interjected out of anger.

When all was said and done, the camera panned the audience.

"Look at those people," Nurse Evans said sarcastically. "They don't even realize they're being bulldozed."

But the words were barely out when something happened to take her breath away. There on the screen, as clear as day, was the young doctor—the one she had left in charge of Ashley Cooper that morning. Feeling the color drain from her face, she turned to Dr. Bishop.

"We need to talk," she whispered hoarsely.

"Mr. Patterson, you have a call on line two."

Jerome Patterson reached down to pick up the telephone, impatiently pushing papers to the side on his messy desk.

"Yeah?" He spoke abruptly.

"Mr. Patterson?"

"Yes?"

"This is Nurse Gina Evans from Mercy Hospital."

He sat up straight in his chair.

"Yes?"

"Remember I told you I would call if I found out anything about Ashley Cooper?"

"Sure. . ."

"Well, I think I have some information you might be interested in. . . ."

He was suddenly very interested.

"Dear Mom. . ."

Cameron held the ink pen in his right hand, poised and ready to write more. If only he could work up the courage to say what he really wanted to say, really needed to say. The pen began to tremble uncontrollably.

"Dear Mom. . ."

Cameron's mother had always loved him. Even when everyone else had turned against him. Even when he had lost the respect of an angry father and the understanding of a younger brother. His mother had remained, if not in action, in spirit.

"I miss you."

He numbly wrote the words, not allowing himself to absorb them. Then, suddenly, they began to tear at him, ripping heart from soul. They weren't strong enough. There were no words to convey the depth of loneliness he was feeling. Months on the street hadn't eased his pain. Relationships, especially the ones on the streets, hadn't helped either. They had only driven him further and further into himself, into his own depression.

"Does anyone love me?"

Had he actually written those words? It was a mistake. That wasn't what he had meant to write at all.

Frustrated, he wadded the paper up into a tight ball in his fist.

"Just catch the ball, Cameron. It's not that hard."

He tossed the wad of paper toward the trash can nearby.

It missed.

"Hey, listen everyone," Mason said, covering the phone with his hand. "Flannigan just held a press conference."

"We missed it?" Abbey asked.

He nodded. "Yes. But turn on the TV anyway. Aaron says Whitener is on now, pitching his side. He's got his lawyers with him."

Shannon's heart skipped a beat. She alone knew what that statement meant. If Paul Whitener was there, Frank would be there. Racing to the den, she flipped on the television set. Others from the house joined her, chattering and talking as if the world weren't about to come to an abrupt end.

There he was, as bold as day, standing with a smile. Nothing in his life was out of order. At least it didn't appear to be. . . .

"You jerk," she muttered. "You hypocritical jerk."

How could he look so calm. . .so normal? Didn't he miss them? Didn't they matter? Suddenly consumed with anger, Shannon reached to snap the television off. No one should see this. No one would see this. . . .

Her hand had no sooner touched the knob than Veronica and Zachary appeared at her side.

"Daddy!" Zachary squealed.

"Daddy's on TV!" Veronica echoed.

Every eye in the room turned to Shannon.

TWENTY-ONE

Look here, Sister," Hannah Gilbert said, staring at the newspaper. " 'Mossy Oaks—Assisted Living with a difference!' Says they've got a pool, two tennis courts, and fine dining."

Molly grumbled from across the room.

"Ooh! And looky here at these two handsome fellas in the picture! One for you and one for me! Now that sounds like just the place for a couple of swingers like us, doesn't it?" Hannah was teasing, of course, but was always looking for a way to cheer her sister up. Why, she couldn't even remember the last time she had seen her crack a smile. Ever since their last serious conversation, things had become very tense in the old, wood-framed house.

The book in question had arrived just yesterday while Molly was napping, and Hannah had carefully disposed of it. Regardless of their situation, there had to be a better solution than the one offered in its pages.

"I can't remember the last time I saw you on a tennis court," Molly answered with a smirk, "and I surely can't imagine those thighs of yours sticking out from under a bathing suit. Surely can't."

"Very funny." It looked like her plan was backfiring. Regardless, Hannah refused to allow herself to be swallowed up in self-pity like her older sister.

"Why is the world are you even looking at that?" Molly asked, frowning. "Read the rest of the paper, why don't you? Why, just look at the headline if you want to see what's really going on out there. It's not all fancy living places and such."

"I never said it was, Molly," Hannah said, shaking her head.

She flipped the newspaper back to the front page. " 'Local couple files injunction to save baby.' " She had already seen the televised version of this story just hours before.

"See what lengths people are having to go to?" Molly mumbled.

"Yes. But it gives us hope, Sister—don't you see?" The story had actually given her reason to think about the future.

"Some hope," Molly mumbled. "The best I can hope for is a swift passing." At this, she paused, mumbling, "I don't know what's taking that book of mine so long to get here."

"You know how the postal service is," Hannah said, avoiding her eyes.

"Well, it's just a matter of time," Molly argued. "Though why anyone would want these old organs of mine is beyond me. My stomach is eaten up with ulcers, and my vision is almost gone."

"You don't have ulcers, Molly," Hannah said sternly. "It's just nerves. And your vision is 20/20!"

"A lot you know! I'm just one step away from death's door, and you're ready to push me through."

"That's ridiculous. You're the one interested in taking the plunge. But I've got a feeling you're going to be with us for a long, long time to come." That would be the inevitable irony of the situation. Molly would probably outlive her.

"Hmph!"

Molly struggled to get up from the recliner. Hannah reached out to help her.

"Don't bother," Molly said. "I've managed on my own this long. I expect I can go on managing. . . ."

Hannah shook her head sadly. There must be something she could do to ease her sister's worry.

172

"Come with me," she said suddenly. "I believe we could use some fresh air!"

"Where are you going?"

"I'm going to the church," Hannah answered. "They're looking for people to help with the bazaar, and we're just the ones to do it."

"Well, maybe you are, but I'm not," Molly tried to argue.

"We're both going," Hannah said, reaching for her purple hat. "And that's that."

Taking her sister by the arm, she swung the door open wide.

Frank shoved the diner door open, forcing his way past the crowd that was trying to make its way outside.

Where was the hostess? There was never anyone to wait on you when you needed it.

Where in the blue blazes is she? Ah, there she is.

"Sorry, Sir, I. . ."

"Three. Table." He spoke the words as a command, never even looking at her.

"Yes, Sir."

Snatching up four menus, she led the way to a table at the back of the diner. It was still dirty.

"I'm sorry, Sir. What about this booth?" She motioned frantically toward a booth in the corner.

"Whatever."

He certainly wasn't in the mood to wait. Then again, he was never in the mood to wait. That's why all this stuff about Shannon had him so crazy. He pressed himself into the booth, feeling a tear in the seat beneath him.

Great.

The waitress stood momentarily, arm extended, as if waiting some command. Frank shoved the menu back toward her. "Just coffee for now. . .black."

There. That should get rid of her.

She picked it up with a grunt. "Yes, Sir."

Walking away rather quickly, she left him to his own thoughts. Frank lit a cigarette, taking a long drag and exhaling with a sigh. A long, loud fit of coughing followed. It was followed by another, directly on its heels. They seemed to be coming more and more frequently these days.

"Excuse me, Sir," a lady from the next booth spoke up. "You can't smoke in here."

He ignored her. The little girl next to her began to cough and wave her arms wildly. Frank was used to this. He had learned to ignore it, too.

"Mommy, that bad man is smoking!" the little girl whined.

"I know, Dear. I asked him to stop"—she turned to glare at him—"but he wouldn't. I guess I'll just have to get the manager."

Frank shrugged. He was far too lost in his own thoughts to worry about anyone else right now. He was thinking about Shannon and the kids—wondering where they were, how they were doing. Had they seen him on TV?

Frank had always been more concerned with climbing the political ladder than spending time with his own family. He knew this—and had even learned to live with it as a matter-of-fact sort of thing. Shannon had her cooking classes, her gardening. She was wrapped up in the kids. He. . .

Well, he was just holding his own until Congressman Paul Whitener decided to call it quits and someone else was needed to fill his seat from this district. That's when all of this agony would begin to pay off.

His heart twisted inside him. For the first time in days, he was beginning to feel guilt. Genuine, honest guilt—not just for what he had said to Shannon—what he had expected of Shannon—but for the role he had played in this whole thing. Watching the Flannigan press conference had done something to him.

"Do unto others as you would have others do unto you."

He could still hear his mother's words. They still stung like a fresh slap. There was some truth there. He couldn't deny that. And he certainly wouldn't want anyone to do back to him what he had done over the last few months. That would be terrible. That would be. . .

No point in thinking about it. What could he do about all of this now? He was in this thing up to his earlobes. Frank broke into another fit of coughing.

"NickStop. Stops the craving." The commercial came on the television overhead just as he managed to catch his breath.

"Have another cigarette, Frank," he muttered to himself. He looked up just in time to see Jerry Morris walk in. Waving, he signaled him. "Jerry!"

Jerry approached, in his usual businesslike way. "Frank."

"Have a seat."

"You're not supposed to be smoking in here," Jerry said.

Frank looked around for an ashtray. Not finding one, he smashed the lit end of the cigarette on the table, then tossed the butt onto the floor at his feet.

The waitress approached, pulling out her pad and waving her hand in front of her face. "It's pretty thick over here, fellas. I could cut it with a knife. Need one?"

"Very funny," Frank said with a smirk.

"You fellas gonna eat, or just sit here and take up space?"

"I'll have the club sandwich," Jerry said, not even looking at the menu.

"And I'll have the spaghetti dinner," Frank added. He had, above all, missed Shannon's cooking. Italian was his favorite.

"We're all out of spaghetti," the waitress said, looking bored. "What about a nice chicken sandwich?"

"Whatever." He shoved the menu back in her direction. He hated chicken.

She marched off, and he turned to look Jerry in the eye. "We've got work to do."

"You'd better believe it," Jerry said. "And I think I've got some news that just might brighten your day."

Jerome Patterson parked his Explorer outside the diner. Snatching a file full of papers, he headed inside. He had important news to share with the gentlemen who had hired him for this rather "sticky" job, and they were waiting inside. He opened the door of the diner.

"Just one?" the hostess asked.

He didn't bother to answer. Sailing past her, he found his party.

"Gentlemen," he said, tossing the paperwork down onto the table, "I believe I have some good news for you."

"Have a seat," Jerry Morris said, motioning.

Jerome sat, flipping the file open. "I believe you will find this very interesting," he said.

"What?" Frank Carpenter asked.

Jerome gritted his teeth before answering. He couldn't stand this man. He had been a thorn in his flesh from the very beginning. Jerome didn't know what it was about him, exactly. Perhaps it was the fact that they were both so much alike.

"I've got a strong lead on one of the intervention groups." He spoke confidently.

"Really?" Frank asked. "Tell me."

"I'm not sure where they're located yet," Jerome said, pulling out a photograph. "But this is the guy we're looking for." He held up a picture of Aaron Landers.

Frank's heart sank to the floor. Aaron Landers. His brother-in-law.

"Name's Landers," Jerome continued, oblivious. "He's a young doctor with quite an attitude about the new law. Seems he's been seen inside Crossings. . .and you'll never guess with who. . ."

"Who?" Frank asked, his heart beating rapidly. Shannon. He was going to say Shannon.

"Ashley Cooper," Jerome said triumphantly. "The missing girl I told you about on the phone." He was gloating now.

"And?" Frank asked, feeling his heart begin to slow a bit.

"And he managed to get her out of Mercy without being seen."

Jerry spoke up now. "One of the nurses saw him on TV—the

day of Flannigan's press conference—and called Jerome."

"How do you know this?" Frank asked, looking stunned.

"I called him this morning." Jerome spoke with a smile, knowing this would be a source of irritation for Carpenter. He always hated being the last to know something.

The scowl on Frank's face spoke volumes. "So now what?" he asked.

"Well, I've got a name and address. It's just a matter of tracking him until he leads me somewhere."

"A safe house?"

Yes. That would explain it. Aaron would lead them to a safe house. Aaron would lead them to. . .

The thought sent a shock wave through him. Aaron would lead them all to Shannon and the kids. Then everyone would know.

"Probably," Jerome responded, looking a little too content with himself. "At any rate, I'm on his tail." He grinned, shutting the folder. "Lunch is on me, fellas."

"Lunch is on me, fellas," Aaron said, holding the diner door open.

He was feeling good today. So good, in fact, that he might even stop by and pick up a dozen yellow roses to carry back up to Havensbrook this afternoon.

Twenty-Two

Would you mind saying that again, please?" Aaron asked incredulously. He had made the trip from the diner to the Fremont Laboratory in Houston's busy medical center in less than thirty minutes—nothing short of a miracle in Houston's inner-city traffic. This was the place where he made his "connection" every week to pick up the SU5368 and other necessary medications for his patients back at Havensbrook.

"I said, 'There's a new drug, even more effective than this,' " the lab technician known only as Ben whispered. "We've been using it for weeks on mice, and it's shrinking tumors twice as fast as this stuff."

"What is it?"

"They're just calling it The Target right now."

"Human tests?"

"Just a few—on those who could afford it. It's been an under-the-table drug for the wealthy. . .those who could buy their way."

"How do I get some?"

"In my opinion, it's still too risky right now. . .too new," the young man continued. "There could be side effects we don't know about yet. I may be able to get you some in about a month or so."

"What about the other thing?"

"The records on the girl?"

"Yeah." Aaron's heart skipped a beat. For days he had waited. He had to get his hands on Ashley's records before they could begin treatment. If they weren't here today, it would mean a full week lost.

"You're in luck, my friend," Ben said, reaching into a drawer and pulling out a hefty file. He pushed it in Aaron's direction. "You must have friends in high places."

"It's not luck," Aaron said, taking it. "But you're right about the other."

He clutched the file tightly, thanking God—and a lab technician by the name of Ben—for it.

"Thank you. It doesn't seem like enough, but it's all I've got."

Ben nodded, turning back to his work.

Aaron nodded. Each day offered more hope. Slipping the file under his coat and the vial of SU5368 into his waiting pocket, he headed for the door.

Jerome Patterson waited in his Explorer just around the corner from Aaron's Jeep. Following him from the diner had been a piece of cake. In fact, this whole thing couldn't have been any easier if he had ordered it up on a silver platter.

"Ah, there you are," he mumbled, watching Aaron exit the laboratory. "I wonder what you were doing in there. . . ."

He turned the key in the ignition, following Aaron's Jeep out onto the busy city street. Wherever he was going, he sure was in a hurry.

Charlotte Tinsdale sat at her son's bedside, stroking his hair.

"Feeling any better?"

He shrugged. Still feverish, he had spent the last several days in bed. Charlotte had been so distracted, she had barely found time to do the work she was elected to do.

"We're going to Houston tomorrow morning," she said, trying to sound as positive as she could. "Did you know?"

179

"Doctor Anderson told me."

"How do you feel about that?" She knew how she felt about it. It made her sick. This was the kind of thing that happened to other people.

"Can Matt come?"

"No. He's got school. But I'll be there on the flight down, and I'll stay with you as much as I can." There was nothing more important to her than that. Nothing. And she wanted him to know it.

"What are they going to do to me?"

Charlotte felt the lump in her throat but tried to push it out of the way. "They're going to run some tests. Doctor Anderson says they've got some of the best heart doctors in the world in Houston. If that's true, then you'll get the best care there."

She didn't speak the words that filled her with dread. Didn't repeat Doctor Anderson's prognosis. It was too hard, too. . .

"Will I have to stay a long time?"

Here she faltered. "I don't know, Babe," she answered quietly. "I hope not."

How could she tell him what she, herself, didn't even know yet? This much she did know—things did not look good for Jonathan.

Ashley stared out the window impatiently. "I thought you said he was coming by three o'clock," she said, turning to Abbey.

"I did. And he will. But what's your hurry? Miss him?"

"Oh, it's not that. . . ."

Ashley couldn't explain the anticipation she was feeling. Part of it, she had to admit, was the excitement of starting the treatment today. The rest. . .

Well, the rest could be due to the fact that she found herself attracted to that redheaded, big-eared, big-nosed, green-eyed lug. Sunday school kid or not. Her heart skipped a beat as she heard the familiar sound of his Jeep pulling up.

"Okay to go out?" she asked apprehensively.

Abbey nodded.

She raced to the door, slowing at its approach. She didn't want to look anxious. Opening the door, she sauntered casually across the lawn. "Hey, what's up?" she asked, as he stepped from the Jeep.

"Not much. Everything," he answered, slipping one arm behind his back.

"Which one?"

"Which one what?" He seemed to be fumbling for words, just like she did.

"Never mind. What's that?" she asked, pointing.

He pulled out an armload of yellow roses, thrusting them at her.

"It's. . .they're. . . I mean, they're for you."

Ashley couldn't seem to wipe the grin off her face, but suddenly it didn't matter anymore. She took the roses into her arms and bounded into the house. . . . "Look what I got!" she hollered for all to hear. "I got roses!"

From around the bend in the road, Jerome Patterson heard it—the sound of a young woman's voice. Picking up his mobile phone, he quickly dialed 911.

TWENTY-THREE

Blaine Bishop sat alone in the cafeteria of Mercy Hospital. It had been a long afternoon, even for him. Two patients in one day—and a blistered conscience was gnawing at him.

"What's up?" Pediatrician Kevin Norwood spoke, pulling up a chair.

Blaine looked up, wishing he had the courage to tell the young doctor to just go away. Courage was not his strong suit. "Oh, not much. Long day."

"Yeah, me too," Kevin said with a yawn. "I fought with the media all morning over that Summerlin baby. They want footage."

"I heard about that," Blaine said, glad for a change of subject. "What's the story?"

"It's just a matter of time. We're waiting it out."

"I mean. . .what's the story with the injunction?" Blaine was more than curious. This was a new tactic many of his own patients were attempting.

"Everything is still tangled up in the courts. We haven't received any word yet. The mother is wearing down some of the nurses—emotionally, I mean. Patients' rights, and all that. . . We've had to ban her from the nursery altogether. That went over like a lead balloon. Now she's got her lawyers fighting us on that, too."

"What's going to happen?" Blaine asked. "Will you have to release the child?"

Kevin shrugged. "I doubt it. The courts are usually on our side. But I guess we'll just have to wait and see. Either way, that kid doesn't stand much of a chance." He glanced down at his watch, then stood abruptly. "I've got an interview in ten minutes. I ought to get going."

Blaine nodded, already deep in thought again. He knew it was just a matter of time before they began losing patients through the injunctions, regardless of Kevin's optimistic attitude.

Patients' rights. He thought about that term a moment. It was outdated, to say the least. The days of patients' rights were clearly in the past—at least for his patients. For some reason, Ashley Cooper came to mind again. He had been plagued with pictures of her for days, nights. . . . He sat quietly, unable to get her off of his mind. Where was she? Was she still alive?

"Murderer!"

The word came again, as clear as a church bell pealing on a summer afternoon. His head instinctively jerked around, looking, wondering. . .

"Murderer!"

There it was again. But it wasn't a real voice. This much he had finally come to grips with. It was the voice of his own conscience, crying out in pain, in guilt.

Guilt.

It gnawed like a rat on a piece of stale cheese. Guilt over the ones he had played a role in selecting for the process, whether ill or not; guilt over the ones who needed a little "finishing off" when the medication hadn't been enough.

"This isn't medicine. This is torture."

Were those his words? Funny, he couldn't seem to get them out of his mind. They irritated him, bothered him. And something else bothered him, too.

His mind flashed back to the other memory—the one that had driven him for years. . . .

"Blaine!" It was the frantic voice of his wife, Susanna, crying from the bedroom.

He made the walk from the living room to the bedroom in silence, knowing before he even entered the room what she would ask, dreading the inevitable.

"You have to help me!" she cried. "It hurts too much. I'm in too much pain!"

Dying a slow death had been painful—for both of them. It had almost killed him to watch her suffer like that. But they had toughed it out longer than most. They had almost made it, almost. . .

"It hurts too much!" Susanna cried. "You have to help me. Do something!"

"But. . ."

"No buts!" she had pleaded. "You know what to do. . . ."

He had, indeed. Blaine reached for a needle, filling it with the clear, deadly mixture. "Thank you! Thank you!" she whispered, trembling as he inserted the needle.

Moments of anguish passed before her eyes closed for the last time. Her last words, "I love you!" hung softly on her pillow.

Blaine still heard them now, and it sent a chill through him.

Aaron smiled at the beautiful young woman seated across from him.

"Okay, now what?" Ashley asked with a laugh. "Am I going to have to have a shot? 'Cause if I am, I think you should leave that part to the nurse."

"What nurse?" Aaron asked, looking around.

There was no nurse in this hidden little place he called a clinic. There was only a small room, a few pieces of necessary equipment, and a precious supply of SU5368.

"Well, if you could afford a nurse," Ashley said laughing.

"Let's don't jump the gun," Aaron said, taking a seat in front of her. "We'll look through your file. And then, well—it just depends. . . ."

He nervously held the file, wishing he had taken the time to look through it before now. If the prognosis was really bad, what would he tell her? What could he do?

"Will we start treatment today?" Ashley asked.

"Probably. Like I said, it just depends."

It did, indeed. Aaron's heart skipped a beat as he flipped the file open. He had promised her the moon. Now all he had to do was deliver it. "You were diagnosed in December, right?" he mumbled, digging.

"Yes. First part."

"Okay. Here are the X rays." He held them up to the light. A wave of adrenaline shot through him. There was nothing on them. Nothing out of the ordinary, anyway.

"Problem?"

"Uh. . ." He stammered, plunging through the file for the other results. What he found nearly knocked him off the chair. His heart was beating doubletime as he spoke: "Ashley?"

"Yeah?"

"Ashley, I. . .I can't be sure, but. . .you don't have cancer."

"What?"

"According to this paperwork, you're not even sick."

Ashley's heart jumped inside of her. "What did you say?" He must be joking. But what kind of a sick joke was this?

"I said," he repeated, "you're not sick."

"That's. . .that's crazy. I was diagnosed. I went for a second opinion. Everyone agreed." She remembered it like it was yesterday. An ordinary well-woman check had turned into anything but when the doctor had extended the examination. The consequences . . .well, the consequences had led her to where she was today.

"Where did they refer you for the second opinion?"

"A specialist. His name was O'Malley." Freckle-faced and good-humored, he stuck in her memory. "Why?"

"I don't see any paperwork with that name. This is too strange." He flipped through the papers more carefully now. "I see a Dr. . . . Can't really make out his name, but it doesn't look familiar to me."

"What?" She saw the expression on his face change.

185

"This is just too strange," he continued, flipping frantically. "The blood types don't even match. And the X rays are. . ."

"Are what?"

"I don't think they're yours. I mean. . .this is a much larger person, with a completely different bone structure."

"Why in the world would they do that?"

"It's. . . It looks like they. . . Hey, have you ever had your appendix out?"

"Of course not."

"Are you sure?"

"Am I sure? Of course I'm sure," she said angrily. "I think I would remember a little thing like that."

"Well, these are definitely not your files then," Aaron said, still flipping. The expression on his face grew more and more concerned as he thumbed through the files.

Ashley's heart suddenly felt as heavy as lead. "What?"

"Which do you want first—the good news or the bad news?"

"Always give me the bad news first," she said, feeling her blood pressure mount.

"This one actually matches your other medical files. They had you typed and matched for organ donation on the day you went into Crossings. You were as good as gone right then."

"What?" She couldn't have heard that right.

"I can't believe they let you slip through the cracks. You were very valuable to them. They had planned to pretty much clean you out."

Ashley felt sick to the very core of her being. "More valuable dead than alive," she muttered.

"But you're not dead," he said emphatically. "You're not even sick! That's the good news."

The wonderful, terrible news. This meant. . .

"You mean, I'm free? . . ." she asked. "I can just walk out of here and. . ."

He interrupted her with a hard stare. "No, Ashley. You don't understand."

"What? All we have to do is show them those papers. . . ."
Now she was angry. Very angry.

"I'm sure it's not that easy," he answered. "We've got to handle this very carefully."

"But. . ." She knew he was right. They still wanted her.

She must have a strategy, a plan. Quietly, she and Aaron sat, deep in discussion, not even knowing the danger that lurked just past the door.

Jerome Patterson pulled his vehicle off of the road, waiting for the police. "No lights. No sirens." That had been his request anyway. To his right—the safe house. Up the road just a half mile or so—a small makeshift clinic with Aaron Landers and Ashley Cooper inside. This was too good.

He looked in the rearview mirror, running a comb through his jet black hair. "There." That should do.

He caught a glimpse of the patrol cars in his rearview mirror as they approached. . .one, two, three, four. That should be just about right. . . . He signaled to the officer in the front car and pulled out onto the road, taking care not to let his tires squeal. They would hit the safe house first. The deed was as good as done.

Mason sat at the head of the table, a prayer of thanks for the dinner fresh on his lips when he heard the sound. It was the sound he had dreaded for months. He looked into the eyes of the others at the table, speaking what his lips could not. They scattered like sheets to the wind.

Cameron raced toward his room, snatching what precious few belongings he still had.

Where is it? Where is it? He groped for the missing picture frame with his mother's photograph. He couldn't leave without it. There was no time to stop and look for missing items now. He would just have to go—and go quickly.

"You're dead to me!"
Yes. He was as good as dead.

Shannon pulled her children close to her—pressing against the paisley wallpaper in the kitchen. She wouldn't run. She couldn't run.

"Do something! Do something!"
They were her own words, a voiceless whisper—echoes of a night three years ago. But as suddenly as they crossed her lips, Shannon understood. Just like that infamous night—there was nothing that could be done. . .and there was no one to blame. Mason was right. It wasn't Aaron's fault.

And complete forgiveness, like a blanket, washed over her— forgiveness for a brother who couldn't have changed things then. . . anymore than he could right now.

TWENTY-FOUR

This is cool, Mom!" Jonathan said, buckling up. "Air Force One."

It did seem rather ironic, Charlotte thought, that her maiden voyage on the famous plane should be to the busy medical center in Houston, Texas. "You're right," she answered, trying to sound nonchalant. "It is cool. In fact, it's downright cold in here."

"Are you trying to make a joke?"

"No," she said, grinning. "Why? Was I funny?"

Charlotte's lips spoke with humor, but her heart spoke otherwise. She was dreading the news that awaited them in Texas. If things looked as bleak as Dr. Anderson had predicted, she might find her own hands tied behind her back, a victim of the very law that now held the country—her country—in its grip.

"I won't let them do it," she whispered to herself. "They're not getting my son."

Coral spoke to the attorney by phone, nearly frantic. "What do you mean?" she asked for the third time.

"I mean," Attorney Joe Harris tried to explain, "that this is just going to take time, that's all."

"The problem is," she said, gripping the dining room table until her knuckles turned white, "we're running out of time."

"Mrs. Summerlin, you don't understand. . . ."

"No, you don't understand," she answered defiantly. There

was precious little time left, and Coral was surer than she had ever been of one thing. She spoke with an anger that seemed to erupt from within: "They're not getting my son."

Jerome Patterson watched the patrol cars pull away from the safe house with a look of pride. Picking up his cell phone, he made the necessary call to Jerry Morris.

"We've got 'em." His words were brief.

He hung up the phone with a grin, knowing that there was still one job left to be done—one that, for personal reasons, he had kept to himself. Up the road, just a half mile or so, were Aaron Landers and Ashley Cooper.

They were his.

Mason Wallis sat in the back of the patrol car, gazing out the window. *So, it's come to this. . . ,* he thought. A sudden wave of despair hit him.

"What have we done to these people?" he whispered. "What have we done?" He reached out for Abbey's hand, gripping it tightly beneath his own.

"God is in control," she whispered.

He squeezed her hand, his only response. Yes, God was in control. But Mason still couldn't stop wondering. . .worrying about Ashley and Aaron. Where were they? Were they safe?

Aaron carefully closed the file, looking Ashley in the eye. He couldn't explain the surge of anger that had crept up on him, but the desire to protect her was stronger now than ever.

"Now what?" she asked.

"Now we go back to Havensbrook for the best pot roast you ever ate. If Abbey's saved us some, that is. . . ."

The sound of tires squealing from up the road caught his ear.

"What was that?" Ashley turned white.

Aaron shrugged. "Maybe Mason. Don't worry."

He glanced out the window, evening shadows playing tricks on his eyes. Was it possible? Could it really be? His eyes fell on an unfamiliar Explorer. His heart instinctively jumped. Something was definitely not right here. He turned back to Ashley.

"What?" she asked, her face draining of color.

"Got your running shoes on?"

"Hurry! Hurry!"

Ashley ran as she had never run before, her heart pounding in her ears. Aaron's loud whisper had all but shattered the stillness of the dense pine forest.

"I'm coming!" she gasped, her own words reverberating through the trees. Just as she spoke, a sharp pain gripped her side. Ashley doubled over, the effects of the cramp leaving her no choice in the matter.

"Stop!" she shouted. "Stop, Aaron!"

His pace slowed as he turned to look at her. "What's wrong?" he asked in a hoarse whisper.

"I can't go any farther," Ashley panted, dropping to her knees. "I. . .can't!"

"But. . ."

"I don't care anymore," she argued, pressing her hands into the painful spot in her side. That was a lie. She did care. But all the caring in the world wouldn't give her the strength to go on. She couldn't.

"Ashley, don't. . ."

She never heard the rest of his admonition. Ashley's heart began to twist inside of her. Heartfelt sobs overtook her, and she collapsed, face in her hands. She truly didn't care anymore. She was lost in a wave of emotion. It rolled over her like a current. She lost all track of time, all awareness of her surroundings. Everything was crumbling. . . . She was breaking. . .breaking. . . .

Tick, tick, tick. . .

Her heart raced in her ears. The memories overtook her. The forest changed its hue. Sepia tones enveloped the trees.

Drip, drip, drip. . .

No! Not that! Her sobs turned to screams, sending a piercing alarm in every direction. *No! Not that, not that. . .that. . .that!* It echoed through the trees hurling back at her.

Drip, drip, drip. . .

She clutched at her arm, trying forcefully to pull the IV out.

But there was no IV. There was only the quiet of the forest—and Aaron. He was here. He always seemed to be here when she needed him most.

"Ashley."

His gentle voice provided a soothing distraction. Where was she again? What was she doing here? And what was it about that voice?

"It's gonna be okay." He sounded so sure of himself, so strong.

Her heart continued to race. Would this never end? And how could it be okay? Would anything ever be okay again? Looking up through her tears, Ashley gazed into Aaron's eyes. There was such kindness there, such peace. Where did it come from?

His arm slipped around her shoulders, comforting her. "Come here," he said. "Lean back on me." Like a child, she obeyed. Ashley felt herself relax in his arms. The tears were still coming, but they were quieter now.

Her thoughts spiraled backward—to the man at the clinic.

"That man. . . He. . .he. . .was looking for me. . . ." She tried to get the words out, but the knot in her throat wouldn't let her.

"Maybe," Aaron said.

"How did he find me?"

"I don't know," Aaron said, his fingers lightly touching her hair.

Ashley sat up quickly, her heart beginning to race again. What had she done? They had to keep moving!

"We've got to get out of here."

"No," Aaron said calmly. "We have to stay here a minute. It's almost dark. He'll never find us out here."

Ashley felt herself begin to relax. She rested in the arms of the man who had now saved her life twice!

"You did it again," she mumbled, her head dropping onto his chest.

"Did what?"

"Rescued me."

"Well, I wouldn't say—"

"I would!" she argued.

For a moment, all was quiet. Then, off in the distance, a flash of headlights. Ashley pressed herself into the darkness. And Aaron, the man whose arms she now found herself in, held her like a little girl. The headlights passed by, moving away from the clinic.

"He's headed to Havensbrook," Aaron said, the fear in his voice more than evident.

"No!" Thoughts of Abbey, Shannon, and the others gripped her.

"We've got to pray."

Pray?

Aaron gripped her hand, praying out loud. It was the first time Ashley had ever heard such passionate words uttered outside the walls of a church. They echoed through the trees. She could actually feel them reaching the heavens.

God? her heart cried out.

"Yes?"

A still, small voice whispered out of the night, touching the very core of her being. Ashley gave herself over to it.

TWENTY-FIVE

W here are they?" Jerome muttered, pulling away from the safe house. Aaron and Ashley weren't here. They weren't back at the clinic either. He shook his head in disbelief. "My lucky night."

Pulling his Explorer back out on the road, he opted to try the clinic one more time. The pull of rubber against the gravel road woke the night.

Maybe, just maybe. . .

"Look. There he goes." Aaron's eyes were fixed on the headlights. Whoever this fellow was, he was headed back to the clinic.

"Your car. . ." Ashley spoke the words into the darkness.

Aaron's car was at the clinic.

"Oh, man. . ." There was evidence in the car—paperwork, maps, plans—anything and everything necessary to send him to jail for a good, long while.

"What are you going to do?" she asked.

"I don't know. But we can't worry about the car right now. Let's just see if we can make it back to Havensbrook." Aaron spoke with all the confidence he could muster.

Taking her hand, they began the precarious journey though brush and bramble. It would have been difficult enough in the daylight, but the cover of night made it almost impossible. "Are you all right?" he asked.

"Yeah."

They traveled in silence for some time. Ashley was quiet. Too quiet. Aaron knew that she was worried.

"It's gonna be okay," he whispered, squeezing her hand. It felt warm, soft. . .comfortable.

A perfect fit.

Ashley clutched Aaron's hand, grateful for the security it brought. Their journey through the woods was nearing an end. Havensbrook was just ahead. Already she could see the lights through Abbey's kitchen window. But what about those inside? Were they safe?

"Let me go in first," Aaron whispered, releasing her hand.

Ashley shook her head frantically, snatching at his arm. She did not want to be left alone in the shadows outside the house. She was still too frightened, too worried. . .

Aaron shook his head. "No."

She responded with an even firmer shake. "Don't leave me!" she whispered loudly.

They pressed themselves against the outside of the house, listening, wondering. . . . There was no sound from inside. That, alone, was a bad sign. This place was always buzzing.

"I'm going in."

Ashley gave him a look, clutching his hand tighter than ever. "Me too."

They slipped in the back door. The kitchen should have been filled to overflowing with houseguests. Instead, it was empty, painfully empty.

"Where did they all go?" Ashley mumbled, shocked.

"I've got a bad feeling about this," Aaron said. "A really bad feeling."

At that moment, Gilligan let out a bark, sending them both into a state of panic.

Aaron reached down to pick up the puppy. "Are you all

alone, fella?" he asked, scratching him behind the ears. He looked around at the empty house. It had been raided. Everyone was. . .

Where would they have taken them? Houston?

For months he had dreaded the possibility of a moment such as this. Now it had come to pass. Mason, Abbey, and all of the others. . . He had put them at risk. This was all his doing.

"It's my fault," he said, placing Gilligan back on the ground. "No."

"Yes. You don't understand." His heart was churning. "I'm the one. . . ."

"What?"

"I'm the one who talked them into using Havensbrook as a safe house." The guilt of those words haunted him. "And now they're—"

Ashley's words stunned him. "They're in God's hands."

He looked up at her, wondering. A glisten of tears in her eyes was almost overshadowed by the position of defense she held. He stood slowly, feeling an odd mixture of happiness and pain.

Before he could help himself, Aaron pulled her into his arms. They stood for what seemed like hours, holding one another.

Ashley's heart was beating madly. She felt so. . .so. . .right in Aaron's arms.

"Are you okay?" she asked, looking up at him.

He nodded, their eyes meeting. She felt his hand reach up to stroke her cheek. Her eyes instinctively drifted shut. She didn't want to let him know how badly she needed his touch. She couldn't let him know. And yet she felt herself pressing her cheek against the back of his hand.

Eyes tightly closed, Ashley never even saw the flash of headlights through the kitchen window, though Gilligan was nipping frantically at her heels.

I'm going to kiss her, Aaron thought, almost as if the words were a question and not a statement of fact. He took her face in his hands, preparing himself for the inevitable, the. . .

All was shattered in a moment. A flash of headlights pulled

him back to reality.

"Ashley!"

She looked up, a mixture of confusion and fear in her eyes. Aaron pointed to the window.

"We've got to get out of here."

Taking her by the hand, they raced to the opposite side of the house.

"They've got to be here," Jerome Patterson mumbled, teeth clenched in anger. He jumped from his Explorer and headed toward the house. A wasted trip back to the clinic had left him in a mood. Of course, it might not be a total waste, considering the paperwork he had pulled from Aaron Landers's vehicle—but without Aaron in custody, it was useless.

He entered through the back door, looking the room over carefully—his eyes like narrow slits. If they were here, he was going to find them.

"Not a bad room!" Charlotte said, turning around.

She and Jonathan had only arrived at Houston's Mercy Hospital an hour ago, and already they were situated in the best private room the hospital could offer. Secret Service men, like magnets, framed the door, the hallway, the elevators. There was a trail of them leading all the way out the front door of the hospital.

"Look. . .cable!" Jonathan shouted, waving the remote as if it were a toy.

"I'm surprised you're not asking for video games," Charlotte muttered, looking at him. "And you don't even look sick, I might add."

"I don't feel sick either. And about those video games. . ."

"No way. Now try to sleep awhile. You need your rest."

He was feeling better today, Charlotte had to admit. It was encouraging but not lasting, according to Doctor Anderson. There would be good days and bad days, or so she had been told. Looked like this was a pretty good one.

TWENTY-SIX

Frank Carpenter turned in early, exhausted from hours of working on the wording of the new bill. In fact, he was nearly asleep when the phone rang. He reached to pick it up, knocking a pack of cigarettes off the bedside table. "Hello?"

"Frank?"

"Yeah."

"Jerry Morris. We need to talk."

"Can't it wait 'til morning?" He groped about in the dark, reaching for the nightstand.

"Definitely not."

Frank flipped the lamp on, squinting its effects away.

"Patterson just called me," Jerry said, sounding excited.

"Yeah?" So what? That guy was all hype and no results.

"He tracked Aaron Landers to a safe house in Gilead. They've arrested fifteen people, including the old man running the place."

Okay. Maybe he was wrong. "Landers, too?" Frank fumbled for the cigarette package.

"No. He's still tracking him—and the Cooper woman."

"When did he call?"

"Just a few minutes ago—from his mobile. He's going to call back as soon as he catches up with them."

"Where did they take the others?" he asked, a cigarette between his lips.

"They're on their way to Houston," Jerry said, "to the downtown jail. I don't know much more than that."

"Should I go?" Frank asked the words, already knowing the answer.

"Paul wants you there to handle the media. He's asked me to stay by the phone in case Patterson calls back. He, uh. . .well, he's busy."

"Right." Great. No sleep again tonight. "Okay," Frank said, pushing the covers back. "I'm on my way."

Only the painful fit of coughing slowed him down.

"Where are we going?" Ashley was panting, her breath hot against the crisp night air.

"I think Mason's old Monte Carlo is out here."

"Where?" she whispered hoarsely.

"In the barn. We planned. . . I mean, we hoped we wouldn't ever have to, but. . ."

"What?"

"We always had a plan," Aaron explained, "in case anything like this ever happened. There would always be a car in the barn with a full tank of gas and keys inside, waiting."

"I hope you're right," she said, the rush of adrenaline forcing her to keep going.

"I hope so, too."

They inched their way across the backyard quietly. Through the kitchen window, Ashley could see the man inside the house. He was tall with slick black hair. A shiver ran up her spine. "Do you know him?" she asked.

"No. At least I don't think so."

Whomever he was, he was certainly determined. His face was tight, drawn. Ashley closed her eyes to block the view.

"We have to keep going," Aaron said, taking her hand.

She followed his lead through the night.

There was something familiar about the man in the house, Aaron thought. Where had he seen that guy before? He couldn't quite place it.

Well, there was certainly no time to stop and figure it out now. Up ahead, just a matter of yards, was the barn. The door, large and looming, should be unlocked, the car ready.

"Dear God," he prayed, "please let it be there."

They approached the side of the barn, easing their way to the door. It opened without a hitch. There, just inside, sat Mason's '81 Monte Carlo. Aaron could barely see it in the shadows that seemed to lurk everywhere.

"That's it?" Ashley asked, stunned. "That's the car we're supposed to drive?"

Even in the dark he could make out the expression on her face. Nodding, Aaron eased the driver's door open. He motioned for Ashley to climb through, putting his finger to his lips. She crawled to the passenger side, the interior light now clearly showing her expression. He followed her, taking his place behind the wheel and gently pulling the door until he heard a little snap.

"Now what?" Ashley asked quietly.

Was that his heartbeat or hers that he heard pounding in his ears?

"We wait," he said, trying to sound like he had maintained some form of composure. "Hopefully he'll give up and just leave. Then we'll make a run for it."

"In this thing?"

"Hey, this is a classic. Mason drives it all the time. . .when he can get it to start, that is."

"Great."

Amazing. Even in the middle of a calamity, she had the capacity to make him crazy. This was a girl worth fighting for.

Jerome Patterson worked his way through the house, gun drawn. He was prepared to do battle with the enemy, at any cost. A clean sweep of the place proved futile. He would have to wait it out in the car.

Crossing the kitchen, he noticed the pot roast and carrots on the table. "Don't mind if I do," he said, filling a plate. He was completely unprepared for the teeth that clamped down on his ankle as he took his first bite.

"What's he doing in there?" Aaron muttered. For nearly fifteen minutes they had waited.

"Maybe he fell asleep," Ashley said with a yawn.

"Surely not. I'm going to go look."

"No. Don't."

"Ashley, it's going to be fine. Just wait here."

Exhaustion must have set in, for she didn't even argue. Aaron eased the door open. He made the short walk to the barn door as quietly as possible.

He stepped out under a moonlit sky, wondering, worrying. He argued with himself about what he was about to do but couldn't seem to change his own mind. He had to get into that Explorer. If this guy had picked up his files, his paperwork—he was doomed.

He inched his way to the vehicle, crouching as low as possible.

"An alarm?" The words crossed his mind, but he let them fall silent. There was no time to worry about that. He approached the Explorer from the passenger side, the safest spot—to his way of thinking.

"Oh, yeah." The keys were in the ignition. The doors were unlocked. "Thank You, Lord!" he whispered.

Slipping the door open was easy, but the ding ding ding that followed nearly gave him a heart attack. "Keys in the ignition, that's all," he muttered, looking at them.

Keys.

The idea was conceived in brilliance—or desperation—he couldn't be sure. On the passenger seat, the files—the papers that would make or break him. Aaron snatched them and ran like a maniac all the way back to the barn.

"What took you so long?"

"I had to get something."

"What?"

He shoved the files in her direction.

"How did you do that?" she asked, shocked.

He held up the keys to the Explorer and grinned. He felt like a hero.

"You are wicked," Ashley said with a smile. "At least he can't follow us."

"If this thing will start," Aaron said, trading keys for key. "Pray, Ashley," he instructed, turning the key to start the Monte Carlo.

Sputter, sputter, sputter. . .

This couldn't be happening.

Sputter, sputter, sputter. . .

"Come on!"

"Why don't we just take his car?" Ashley asked, nerves showing.

"I don't want to have to do that. . . ." Aaron said, feeling guilty even thinking about it. "That would be stealing."

"Man, you really are a Sunday school kid, aren't you?"

He nodded.

"Did it ever occur to you that taking his keys was stealing, too?"

He shook his head.

"Well, hello!"

"I'm trying not to think about it. Now be quiet."

Sputter, sputter, sputter. . .

"Please!" Their voices rang out in unison.

Sputter, sputter, sputter. . . Purrrr. . .

Thank God!

Aaron placed the car in gear, headed for the barn opening. Just as he passed from the cover of darkness into the moonlight, a shadow fell across his path.

A shot rang out in the dark.

"Where are you taking my children?" Shannon all but screamed the words. "They haven't done anything wrong!"

"They're just being taken to the juvenile holding facility

until another family member arrives." The deputy wasn't speaking out of cruelty. He was just doing his job. "Is there someone we can call?"

"Yes." Shannon spoke hesitantly. "My husband. You can call my husband." She avoided the officer's eyes at all cost. "Tell him. . ." She fought the lump in her throat to speak the words. "Tell him we're home."

Home.

The word, itself, no longer even sensible. None of this made sense. Had she risked losing one child only to end up losing all three?

"I'll pass that word along," the deputy said, looking sympathetic. "How do I reach your husband?"

"His name is Frank Carpenter," she said quietly. "He's probably at home right now, sleeping. I can give you the number."

"Frank Carpenter?" the deputy asked, looking stunned. "Frank Carpenter, the attorney? The one who works for the congressman?"

"Yes. Why?"

"Lady, you're not gonna believe this. . . ."

She didn't.

Blaine Bishop tossed and turned on the bed like a man tormented. He was a man tormented.

"Murderer!"

The children cried from silhouetted caskets.

"Murderer!"

The elderly screamed out from beyond granite tombstones.

"Murderer!"

The sick and infirm echoed with hollow, empty voices.

"I love you!"

His darling Susanna cried out in anguished pain.

Waking abruptly, Blaine began to shake. "I can't take this anymore!" he cried out to the darkness. Dr. Bishop was ready— ready for anything that might stop the pain that consumed his days and nights.

TWENTY-SEVEN

Jerome Patterson barely had time to catch his breath. Shivering in the cold night air, he watched the Monte Carlo drive on.

"Time to get back to the shooting range," he mumbled. His aim in the shadowy darkness was not what it should have been.

It was of little consequence. He was now hot on their tails. It was just a matter of time. Jerome tore like lightning across the yard, yanking the door of the Explorer open.

"You're mine, Aaron Landers," he mumbled, reaching for the keys. . . . The keys?

Frank Carpenter arrived at the jail, completely unprepared for the awful truth that met him there.

"You've got to be kidding me."

His wife and children were waiting inside. A mixture of relief and anger swept through him at first. The relief passed quickly, anger now fully encompassing him. He was going to give Shannon a piece of his mind, and then, when he took her back. . .*if* he took her back, she would never think of trying anything like this again.

"Do you realize the risk you've put our children in?" Frank shouted, eyes fixed on Shannon's.

"Our children?" she responded numbly. "I was doing this for our children."

"That's ridiculous. You have to see that."

"I couldn't kill the baby," she answered, her eyes looking glassy from lack of sleep. "That's all there is to it."

"It was never your choice."

"That's what worried me," she whispered. "Don't you get it?"

He felt his heart give a little, watching a tear slip out of her eye. She could always get to him with those tears.

Shannon sat across the table from Frank, shaking like a leaf. He had spent the better part of the last half hour shouting at her, threatening her.

"But Frank. . ." She tried to get a word in edgewise. It was futile. Tears raced like rivers down her cheeks.

Mason sat quietly in the jail cell, praying. Somewhere his wife and the other women were being questioned. The Havensbrook men had already been through the wringer. For his part, he had said nothing—absolutely nothing—which had infuriated the officers to no end.

Like a lamb led to slaughter. That's how he felt. He turned to look at Cameron, sleeping on the bed just across from him. The young man had maintained a cold silence all the way from Havensbrook. Where was his heart? What was he thinking, feeling now?

Was there any reaching him?

Cameron lay quietly in the bed, trying not to disturb Mason. Best to feign sleep. He trembled beneath the blanket the officer had thrust through the bars. It wasn't cold in here. He was terrified.

What will they do to me? The question rolled around his head, over and over. But he knew the answer—knew what they would do. He would have thirty days, and then. . .

He couldn't think about the then part of it. He wasn't ready. *Ready for what?* Another question to answer.

Ready to face the inevitable! Ready to face. . .God? Was there really a God? When Cameron looked into the piercing eyes of Mason and Abbey, he could almost believe it. . .almost. . .

But, no! What kind of a God would allow him to get sick? What kind of a God would turn his parents against him? What kind of a God would have created the chaos in his mind about his own identity?

"Mom. . ." He spoke the word in a half whisper. Maybe tomorrow he could call her, tell her what was happening. Maybe tomorrow he could. . .

"You are dead to me!"

The angry face of his father appeared suddenly, just across the jail cell. Cameron sat up, gasping.

"Dad?" His voice was trembling, an outward expression of inward terror. Just as suddenly, the face disappeared.

"Cameron?" Mason spoke out of the darkness. "Cameron, are you okay?"

Okay? His life was over.

The drive from Havensbrook to Houston seemed to drag on for an eternity. Ashley sat in the Monte Carlo, forcing herself to stay awake all the way, though her eyes were weighted with the events of the night.

Gunshot.

The sound of it still echoed in her ears. But here they were, safe and sound, headed to. . . "Where are we going?" she asked, worried.

"I can't take you to my apartment," Aaron answered, sounding as tired as she felt. "That's the first place they'd look."

"What about my mom's?"

"I don't think so," Aaron answered. "They're probably already watching her."

The thought of it made Ashley sick.

"I wouldn't even call her, if I were you," Aaron continued. "I'm sure the phone is tapped."

Ashley nodded, overwhelmed by an urgency to sleep. "I'm so tired."

"I know. I think I'm going to stop."

"Where? Where are we?"

"Just north of The Woodlands," he said, pointing. "I know there's a hotel about a mile or so from here. We'll stop and get some sleep. I don't know about you, but I'm worn out."

"Finally," she whispered, her eyes drifting shut.

Aaron left the car running while he went inside the motel office. Ashley was nearly asleep now. They had to rest. No one could go on at this pace. And what safer place than this? I-45 was crowded and under construction, as always. People by the thousands passed by, never taking the time to notice anyone else.

He emerged from the lobby, moments later, keys in hand.

"We're on the second floor," he said, slipping back into the car, "in the back."

She nodded. "Mmm-hmm. . ."

It would be safer, he had concluded, to park as far from the street as possible. The cover of night was a temporary protection, but only temporary. He knew it was just a matter of time before the police noticed the Monte Carlo.

Aaron had to work like the dickens to get Ashley up the stairs. She had already given herself over to the exhaustion.

"Here we are," he said, putting the key in the door. He pushed it open, a tiny room with two double beds inside.

"I'll take that one over there," he said, pointing to the far wall.

It didn't matter. She had already tumbled, clothes and all, onto the nearest one.

"Ashley?"

He felt sure she never heard him through the snoring.

TWENTY-EIGHT

Cardiomyopathy?" Charlotte Tinsdale pondered the word, the bright Texas sun almost blinding her through the cracks in the venetian blinds.

"It's a fairly serious illness," heart specialist Morgan Keenan explained. "The heart muscle becomes inflamed for one reason or another—usually as a result of a viral infection."

Charlotte's mind raced back over the months. Jonathan had struggled with a pretty serious viral pneumonia less than six months ago. It had been a rough two weeks, but this? . . .

"The symptoms are. . . Well, you've lived with them for the last few days, so I'm pretty sure you've figured it out—shortness of breath, dizziness, abnormal heart rhythms. Some secondary infections, perhaps."

"How serious are we talking here?" Charlotte asked, wanting the truth.

"Very serious, I'm afraid," Dr. Keenan said, looking her in the eye.

Charlotte glanced at Jonathan in the bed, half asleep after a fitful night of tossing and turning. "Let's finish this conversation out in the hall."

"No, Mom." Jonathan spoke, her first indication that he had been listening. "I want to know."

He was apparently much braver than she was.

"Go ahead," Charlotte said, nodding in the doctor's direction.

"Well, Jonathan's heart cavity has become enlarged as a result," he continued, "and then weakened. It doesn't pump normally, and—"

"And?" She wanted to know.

"I don't want to alarm you, Madame President, but in situations like this, congestive heart failure often follows."

Charlotte felt her own heart begin to fail. This was far worse than she had expected. "What are we talking here?"

"Transplant."

The president of the United States felt her knees give out from under her. This couldn't be happening. She wasn't strong enough.

"No! We can't. . . I can't. . ."

"It's okay, Mom," Jonathan spoke from the bed. "I can handle it."

His words electrified her. If he could handle it, she could handle it.

"What do we do first?" she asked, looking at the doctor.

"Well," Dr. Keenan said, looking at the ground. "That's where we run into a little problem. . . ."

"You can't leave me here," Ashley said, staring up at Aaron. She had slept like a log all night, only to wake to this.

"I have to, Ashley," he said. "I've got an appointment with Congressman Flannigan at 11:30 at the Medical Center, and it's too dangerous to take you there. The president is there. In fact, Flannigan is meeting with her at noon."

"The president?" she asked. "Why?"

"Her son is sick."

"Which son?"

"Jonathan, I think."

"What's wrong with him?"

"I don't know. I just know he's at Mercy."

Her heart began to pound instinctively.

"Mercy? Of all places, why there?"

"I don't know. But I'm sure all of that will come out in the wash," Aaron said. "I've got to go."

"I don't like this!" she argued, fear rising. "The whole place will be swarming with secret service, and every deputy in Harris County will be there."

"I'm a big boy. I'll be okay."

"And I'm a big girl," she said, standing, "So I'm coming, too." The thought of entering Mercy Hospital sickened her, but she couldn't let him go through this alone—not for her. . . .

"No way. Now stay here. Don't call anyone. Don't go anywhere—not even to the restaurant."

"I'm starving! I didn't get any dinner last night."

"I brought you this." He tossed a package of cinnamon rolls and a diet soda onto the bed.

"Thanks." Her knight in shining armor.

"No problem. Got them early this morning. You were out like a light."

She shrugged. "I was tired."

"Did anyone ever tell you that you snore?"

"I do not!" Was he kidding? It was hard to tell from the look on his face.

"Hmm. Well, let's just say the walls were vibrating."

Now she was hot. "You're making that up."

"I wish I were," Aaron said, yawning. "I was up all night. Couldn't sleep a wink."

"That's not funny." Ashley glared in his general direction. If Aaron Landers thought any of this was funny, he had another thing coming.

"I'll be back by 2:00," Aaron said, closing the door with a grin.

The look on her face was worth every moment of teasing. Aaron had barely resisted the urge to sweep her into his arms. Too much was happening, and too fast. He wanted to make sure she was ready for a relationship before tossing it into her lap.

Scoping the parking lot, Aaron made his way over to the Monte Carlo. It started like a charm. "Oh, sure!" he mumbled.

"Today you start."

He made the journey to Mercy Hospital, deep in thought. Meeting with Flannigan wasn't going to be easy, especially with police and secret service personnel all over the place.

"I don't want to put you at risk." He had warned Flannigan over the telephone. But, always the gentleman, the congressman had brushed away his fears. "Meet me at 11:30. My car will be in the west parking lot."

It was 10:50 now. He glanced down at his watch, almost losing control of the car. "Come on now," he mumbled to himself.

Traffic was worse than usual this morning. An accident on 59 South almost made him late. Aaron pulled into the west parking lot at 11:31. A blue Explorer. That shouldn't be too hard to spot. No, there it was. . .right over there.

Aaron eased the old Monte Carlo up to the waiting spot next to Flannigan's vehicle.

"Glad you could make it." Flannigan was smiling.

"Not as glad as I am," Aaron said. "I've got something to show you."

He pulled out Ashley's file, passing it with trembling hand to the congressman.

"What's this?"

"Proof. Proof that Ashley Cooper never had cancer in the first place. Proof that Mercy Hospital is working under the table. Proof that the government is backing them."

"You're kidding. . . ."

"No, I'm not."

Flannigan thumbed through the stack of papers carefully. "I'll have to take your word for it. I don't understand any of this medical lingo."

"Doesn't matter," Aaron said bluntly. "You can bank on it. She's not sick. Never was—and I'm convinced she's not the only one. If you could get access to hospital files, I'm sure you would find others."

"Consider it done." Flannigan spoke with confidence. "I'll pass this along to the attorneys. It should be enough to clear Ashley's name. But we've still got so much to do with the others. . . ."

"Tell me," Aaron said. He had waited and wondered all night long. He had to hear about Mason, Abbey, Shannon, and the others.

"They're in the downtown jail."

He had figured as much. "The kids?" He had been particularly worried about them. Foster care would be the county's only option if Frank couldn't be located.

"Their father picked them up in the middle of the night."

"I guess that's for the best." Frank Carpenter wasn't a very nice man, but he had always been good to his children.

"Tell me about Shannon." His heart ached, thinking of his sister. He wanted to go to her. He wanted to talk to her.

"She's pretty bitter, I think," Flannigan said. "I had a chance to talk to Mason last night, and he expressed some concerns about her."

Wasn't that just like Mason. . .to be sitting in a jail cell thinking about someone else's feelings? He was still the same amazing man he had always been. Nothing would ever change that.

"What happens next?"

"Well, I've got attorneys willing to file injunctions, but I don't know how quickly we can move, or if the fact that these folks have already been arrested will make an injunction impossible. We've been told they're transporting many of them right here— to the Crossings wing of Mercy."

It sent a shiver up Aaron's spine. He couldn't help but think about his last visit here, less than two weeks ago. It was the first time he had ever laid eyes on Ashley Cooper.

"And speaking of Mercy," Flannigan continued, "I'd like to meet with you after this is all over so that we can formulate a plan of action for you, personally. Don't want to see you end up behind bars. Can you wait?"

"Here?"

Flannigan nodded.

Aaron shrugged. "I don't know. I left Ashley alone."

"I'm sure she'll be fine," the congressman said with a smile. "She sounds like a pretty sensible girl."

Ashley hailed a cab from the corner in front of the motel. A pair of dark sunglasses and a scarf over her hair were her only attempts to disguise herself.

"Where to, Ma'am?" the driver asked.

"Medical Center. Mercy Hospital." Even the words gave her a chill. But there was someone at the hospital who might be able to help her. The president of the United States was in Houston this morning. Ashley was going to get to her if it was the last thing she ever did.

"They're going to release you," Frank Carpenter explained, "on the condition you abort the baby within thirty days."

How could he even imagine she would be willing to do that? Shannon's heart broke just thinking about it. "Frank. . ." But there was no arguing with him. The best thing to do, she decided, was to just go along with him for the moment. The future could take care of itself.

"What about the others?" she asked.

"What about them?"

"Isn't there anything you can do?" Surely a man in his position could do something.

"Why? They broke the law."

"It's a dumb law." Her words were short but to the point.

He glared at her, eyes like arrows. "It's a law I helped write."

Shannon shrugged. Sometimes the truth hurt.

TWENTY-NINE

Madame President. . ."

"Please, call me Charlotte." She stared at the young congressman. "I've heard so much about you."

"All good, I hope!" Congressman Flannigan said with a smile.

"All good."

"Madame Pres. . .I mean Charlotte, I'd like you to meet Jacob and Coral Summerlin. Their son is here at Mercy."

"Oh, I'm sorry!" She could certainly empathize. "What's wrong with him?"

"No, I'm the one who's sorry," Flannigan said, looking flustered. "I should have made myself clear. What I meant to say was—their son is in the Crossings wing at Mercy Hospital."

"Oh." How could she possibly respond to that? What did one say in a situation such as this? She extended her hand, grasping Coral's. "What's wrong with him?"

"Down's syndrome."

Charlotte shook her head. "We've got to stop this. Things are completely out of control."

The congressman nodded. "There is good news, though. We filed an injunction. The judge just gave us her decision this morning at 9:15. They're going to release the baby to the parents—at least temporarily."

"Let me be there when it happens," Charlotte said, standing.

214

"I have to see this for myself."

"That's exactly what I was hoping you would say," Flannigan said, smiling.

Charlotte's heart felt like it was on fire. The Duty to Die law had stretched itself out across the miles of American soil, sweeping innocent victims into the wake of its violent storm. "I'm going to stop this thing," she stammered. "I have to stop this thing."

Coral's heart nearly exploded within her. Jamie was finally coming home! She stared across the room at this woman—the president—her president, and felt such sympathy for her. Her son was gravely ill. She might lose him. Coral, of all people, knew how that felt.

The tears burst suddenly, like a dam. She reached across the divide to embrace the frightened woman who held the fate of so many in her frail hands.

"God will help you." Coral's words were whispered.

"I believe He will," came the awaited response.

Shannon paced the living room, trying to decide what to do. She and Frank had arrived home only moments before. The children were down for naps, Frank had just left to meet with Paul Whitener, and she found herself very, very alone.

The last thing she wanted to be right now was alone.

"This may be the end of our working relationship."

Frank heard Paul Whitener's words but scarcely believed them. "Why?"

"You withheld information from me about your wife and children. You used my name to get her released. You can't be trusted. It's that simple."

"But. . ."

"There are no buts here, Frank. Either you're on the team or you're not. Apparently you're not."

Frank stood silently, shaking his head. It was suddenly very clear—he was not on Paul Whitener's team.

And it felt awfully good.

"Happy birthday to you! Happy birthday to you! Happy birthday, dear Molly. . . Happy birthday to you!" Hannah sang out loudly, struggling to keep from dropping the large chocolate cake she carried. Like a blazing campfire, sixty-eight candles sat perched atop the beautifully decorated work of art.

Hannah had worked all afternoon on it. The tiny dining room in the old Gilbert home was filled with fellow church members adding their voices to hers in joyful chorus. Their smiles and laughter were almost contagious.

Almost.

"I said no party!" Molly grumbled under her breath, a forced smile upon her lips. "I was just hoping to forget about my birthday this year."

"Pooh!" Hannah argued. "Why, I would never forget your birthday! Never have, never will!"

Molly feigned a smile, greeting one of the guests. Hannah went on about her business, gathering the people around her like so many chicks around a hen. "Come on, everyone! It's time for Molly to blow out the candles!"

Her older sister groaned loudly, almost interrupting the moment.

Almost.

"Go on, Molly," Hannah whispered, giving her a little nudge.

"You'll be the death of me yet, Hannah Gilbert," Molly whispered. "Why, with my asthma, it'll take the last bit of air in me to get these candles blown out."

"You don't have asthma, Molly," Hannah whispered back. "Now blow out the candles before I pour a bucket of water over you and that cake."

Molly obligingly leaned down and blew.

And blew.

And blew.

It took awhile, but she finally got them out. A roar went up from the crowd, and for the first time in days, Hannah actually thought she saw Molly smile.

Almost.

Jerome Patterson pulled his rental car up to the parking lot of Mercy Hospital. He was on a mission. Something in his gut just told him that Aaron Landers would be here today.

Patterson's eyes were open, scanning the parking lot for the old Monte Carlo that had almost run him down last night.

"Where are you?" he muttered.

THIRTY

Are we ready?" President Charlotte Tinsdale asked, looking at Congressman Flannigan carefully.

"Yes." He answered with a smile.

Charlotte hated to leave Jonathan alone in the hospital room, but this was important—very important. Besides, there were enough secret service men outside to protect ten or twelve boys his age.

"Ladies and gentlemen, the president of the United States."

She approached the podium in Mercy Hospital's lobby with great anticipation.

"My fellow Americans," she began. No, that sounded too formal. "Friends, I have asked for this opportunity to speak with you about an issue that concerns us all."

There was a hush in the lobby. It was deafening.

"My son Jonathan, as you know, was just diagnosed with cardiomyopathy, a degenerative heart condition." She looked out into the eyes of those in the room. There was compassion there. She continued courageously. "I know that the doctors spoke with you a short while ago, but I felt compelled to add to their words."

She looked out over the group, preparing herself for the words that needed to be spoken, praying for the courage to speak them.

"I have shared my feelings about the Duty to Die law on

other occasions. I am concerned that many of you may think I am speaking this way simply because my son is ill. I assure you, that is not the case. I believe. . . ," here she paused. "I should say—I join with the millions of Americans who believe the law is unconstitutional."

A murmur rose, filling the lobby. She watched the expressions on the faces of doctors, nurses, and others on the hospital staff turn from compassion to concern. She had gone from being a friend to a foe in one short statement.

"And yet—here I stand," she continued, "in the lobby of one of the greatest hospitals in our country, bearing the name Mercy, fighting for the right to save my own son's life."

Concern turned to whispers and cold stares.

"My son's condition, as you heard, is not good. The fact that he needs a heart transplant to survive may place him within the confines of the new law. In other words, the transplant might not take place—simply because of the law itself. This fact, like so many others related to the Duty to Die law, compels me to continue in my quest to see it overturned. Will you join with me?"

The murmur in the lobby rose slightly. Some were nodding. Others were shaking their heads. Charlotte bravely continued on: "Death does not discriminate. Why should we? Is it feasible to think we can return to a time when a healthy respect for life—all life—is possible? I hope so. I pray so."

She looked to her right. Coral and Jacob Summerlin were waiting, a look of frantic anticipation in their eyes. They would get their turn at the microphone next. Their plight was not so different from hers, really. They were just parents who loved their child and were willing to risk everything to save him.

"Why, then, are we facing a law that forces death on those who are not yet ready for it?" she continued. "When did we become God? And if we're not—then why should we even be discussing such things?"

The audience looked very nervous indeed. But Charlotte wasn't shaken. She had passed nervousness several sentences back. She was driven by the look of determination she had seen on Jonathan's face just before leaving his hospital room.

"Some would argue that keeping terminal patients alive is the equivalent of 'forcing' them to suffer. I would have to disagree. Death, like life itself, is a process—and its time is ordained by God. The Bible tells us—'There is a time to be born, a time to die. . . .' "

This would create an automatic argument, but why not forge ahead now that she had gone this far?

"Who are we to force the hand of an almighty God? Yet that is exactly what we seek to do when we send someone to an early death—whether against his or her will—or with it. Sadly, we are causing them to miss out the final stage of growth in their own lives, both emotionally and physically. Who are we to rob them of that?"

Who, indeed?

"There is an equal-protection clause in the Fourteenth Amendment. Any law that seeks to restrict our constitutional rights as citizens is subject to examination. Any such law can—should—be struck down."

She believed it with her whole heart, and she was going to play a part in making it happen. The history books would prove it.

"Now let me speak to you about a word that has been missing from the Duty to Die equation. That word is hope. How quickly we forget that many people actually recover from life-threatening illnesses. Medications are available. Doctors are obtaining knowledge. But even when individuals face the inevitable, we must remind ourselves that they still have something left to offer their families, their loved ones. They have stories, history—and wisdom. Offering patients hope would include giving them the right—the time—to pass those things along. And we seem to have forgotten in the midst of this that we can and should pray. Have we really, as a society of people, neglected our belief in the miraculous?"

She spoke with passion, her heart full. This was more than just a simple message to the masses. This was her heart. This was her conviction. This was her. . .calling. Yes, calling. And Pete would have been proud. Very proud.

Charlotte continued bravely on, pressed with new determination. "If the 'process' of death is properly managed, we offer hope to families, providing them not only more time together, but the opportunity to care for a loved one when that loved one needs them the most. This should be our mission—our goal. It's a critical part of who we are as human beings—caring for one another. The problem is, we've always been so eager to 'get things over with' that we often lose sight of the truth—life is precious."

She smiled in Coral's direction, knowing that she had a friend, an ally.

"All of life is precious. And, along those lines, I would like to introduce my new friends, Coral and Jacob Summerlin. They have something they wish to say."

Coral approached the microphone, shaking like a leaf. It wasn't just the fear of speaking before the nation, it was the fact that—rounding the corner—was her infant son, in the arms of a Crossings nurse. She was about to hold him for the first time since that wonderful, terrible day in the delivery room. What could be more important than that?

"Less than two weeks ago," she began, looking more at the baby than the camera, "the Lord blessed my husband and me with a beautiful son. He was born here at Mercy Hospital. We named him Jamie."

"If it's a boy, we'll name him James Daniel. . . ."

She looked at the infant, who had just been passed from the nurse's arms to those of President Charlotte Tinsdale. Coral felt the familiar lump in her throat again.

"Jamie was born with Down's syndrome. In the eyes of the new law, he is defective. To my husband and me, he is perfect."

The tears slipped down her cheeks, anxiety growing.

"We were told right away that Jamie would be. . . Well, there's no easy word for it. Jamie would be killed. He had no choice in the matter. We had no choice in the matter. None of us had a voice, though we cried from the rooftops. . . ."

Brushing the tears away, she continued.

"We looked for help and found it—in prayer, in a bold congressman by the name of Flannigan, and in a host of attorneys who worked tirelessly on our behalf. I want to encourage those of you who want a second chance to do the same."

Here she smiled.

"We just received word today that a temporary injunction has been granted. Baby Jamie is coming home with us—at least for the time being."

A gasp went up from the crowd as the infant, her beautiful, perfect son, was placed into her arms.

The sweet smell of talcum power tugged at her heart. Two precious eyes, a tiny little nose, the blue bonnet—they all ran together in the magic of the moment as she planted kisses on his forehead. Her son was alive. Her son was safe.

Unable to speak, Coral stepped away from the microphone.

Dr. Blaine Bishop stood at a great distance, trying to make sense of the words that had just been spoken. The guilt that had plagued him for months was now unstoppable. It consumed him.

Ashley jumped from the cab, waving to the driver. "I'll have to go inside to get your money."

"Aw, come on lady!"

"No, really. I'll be right back." She breezed through the door, past two guys in black suits, completely unprepared for what awaited her on the other side.

"Hold it right there."

"Huh?"

An army of police officers stood just inside the door. One tugged at her arm, almost angrily. "Where do you think you're going?"

"I, uh," she stammered. "I'm here to see the president."

Aaron sat in the Monte Carlo watching, waiting for Flannigan's arrival. Just yards away, at the hospital entrance, a young woman was exiting a cab.

She looked like. . . No, it couldn't be!

THIRTY-ONE

Charlotte passed the baby to the waiting arms of his mother, feeling a pull at her heart like she had never known. Right now, all she wanted was to get back up to Jonathan's room, to hold him. . . to tell him how much she loved him.

But the cameras were on her now, and she knew how important this moment was. Placing Baby Jamie into Coral's arms was a symbolic move of solidarity. They were on the same team. Millions were on the same team. Millions were. . .

A woman's voice pealing out through the lobby interrupted her thoughts. . . . "Madame President! Madame President!"

What in the world? . . .

Secret service men, like so many flies, buzzed around her. Voices were raised. Guns were raised.

"What's happening?"

Off in the corner she could see a young woman, blond curls, wire-rimmed glasses, pressed against the wall, surrounded by officers and secret service agents. Who was she? Why was she here?

Ashley could see her—just across the lobby—the president of the United States.

"I just need to talk to her!" she shouted to the men in black.

They held her tightly against the wall, guns pointed in her face. Looking up, she saw Aaron enter, his eyes wide.

Oh no. This was not quite how she had planned it. Her eyes roamed the crowd, looking for a friend.

Blaine Bishop.

Dear God, no!

Aaron slipped right through the door and into the lobby of Mercy Hospital, completely unseen. Police and secret service men were so distracted by Ashley that he didn't even exist—at least not yet.

There she was, pressed like a common criminal against the wall. It was only a matter of time.

Jerome Patterson watched the chaos from outside the hospital door. No way was he going in there. Turning quickly, quietly. . .he headed back to his car.

Coral watched with great fear. Who were these people? Were they here to hurt her—to take her baby? She wasn't going to let that happen. Not again! But wait. . . Wasn't that the young doctor, the friend of Congressman Flannigan's?

Blaine's heart felt like it was leaping from his chest.

Ashley Cooper. She was very much alive. From across the room, their eyes met. He watched all of the color drain from her face, like hope from the once-hopeful.

"So," he whispered to himself, "that's the effect I have on people."

"Murderer!"

The crowd roared the words.

Blaine closed his eyes, trying to shut them out.

"Murderer!"

He was surrounded on every side.

And yet, he wasn't either. Everyone was wrapped up in the madness of the moment. No one was even looking at him.

Turning, he walked the other way.

President Charlotte Tinsdale heard Congressman Flannigan's voice above the roar. Even through the sea of secret service men surrounding her, she could tell he was trying to speak to her.

"They're with me!" he was shouting.

Aaron searched the crowd, looking for Flannigan. There he was, near the president. But could he get to him? He worked his way through the crowd until his hand reached Flannigan's sleeve.

"Thanks for waiting in the car." They were the congressman's only words, and they were more than a little short.

"I'm sorry. I was. But Ashley. . . She showed up. I saw her come in, and I thought. . ."

"Thought you wanted to be the hero?" Flannigan asked, now smiling. "Can't blame you there. Seems like it's in your blood."

The roar of the crowd was diminishing. Ashley now stood silently against the wall. The president stood silent within the circle of safety provided her. The Summerlin family stood quietly off to the side.

"Get them out of here." He heard the president's words. The media began to scatter.

"Heavens to Betsy, Sister. . . Did you see that?" Hannah pressed as close to the television as possible.

"Well, I heard it!" Molly exclaimed. "But I can't see a thing through that big rear end of yours. You're blocking my view."

Hannah pulled away from the set slightly to allow her sister more room.

"That's the most amazing thing I've seen in all my born days," she said.

"Better than the soaps," Molly agreed. "Better than the soaps."

THIRTY-TWO

Who is she?" Charlotte asked. "What does she want?"

"I believe I can answer that, Madame President." Aaron heard his own words, scarcely believing them.

"Who are you?" She looked the young man over carefully. He was not familiar, though he appeared to be friendly with Flannigan.

"My name is Aaron Landers. . . ." He knew the words would come with a price. "I've been working with an underground intervention group, rescuing waiting patients from an early death. This is one of the patients I, uh, kidnapped. . .from the Crossings wing of this hospital less than two weeks ago."

"Really?" That certainly got her attention. And all of this in front of an audience.

"Yes, Ma'am. I believe she would like to speak with you about the Duty to Die law."

Charlotte's eyes met those of the young woman at the wall. She was frightened, eyes huge. The president of the United States knew just how she felt.

"I want to talk to you!" she said, pointing. "And you, too." Her finger hit Aaron squarely in the chest.

"But Madame President," the secret service men argued.

"Give them clearance," she instructed. "This is very important." She didn't care what it took. She was going to get to the bottom of this.

Ashley's eyes still pleaded for help.

"Let her go!" Charlotte felt the strength of her words, bellowing out across the lobby.

They did. She tumbled like a rag doll to the floor.

"Meet me upstairs in twenty minutes," Charlotte said defiantly. "I need to spend some time with my son, if you don't mind."

Mason Wallis paced the jail cell, deep in thought. Cameron lay on the cot across from him in complete silence.

"You can't stay shut up like that forever," Mason said finally. "We need to talk about this."

"Talk about what? There's nothing left to talk about."

"Yes, Cameron. There is."

How could he make the young man understand that this life, no matter how long or short, was futile if you were not prepared for the one to come?

Shannon sat glued to the television, not believing her eyes. There was her brother—for the whole world to see—creating chaos in the lobby of Mercy Hospital.

She shook her head. "Aaron. What in the world are you doing?"

But it was obvious. He was there to help Ashley. Forever the rescuer, Aaron would continue risking his life. What gave him the courage? What gave him the. . .

Her thoughts were temporarily interrupted. The television screen went black. All cameras shut off, the scene just disappeared —like a puff of smoke.

"Hey, what happened?"

A news reporter began to speak, trying to make sense out of what had just happened.

"Today, in the lobby of Houston's busy Mercy Hospital, the president of the United States risked her life to speak to a waiting public. . . ."

But Shannon was lost in her own thoughts. The courage that spurred Aaron on, she knew, came from a faith—something deep inside him. She had known it once. She would know it again.

And this baby would know it, too.

"What did you think you were doing?" Ashley heard Aaron's words and looked up at him. She was still sitting on the floor, afraid to move, afraid to breathe.

"I, uh, I don't know."

"That's pretty obvious."

"I thought I might get to talk to her," Ashley said, tears rolling. "I thought she, of all people, would understand—maybe she could do something to help me—to help the others. But she wouldn't know if I didn't come. . . ." Didn't he understand? She just wanted all of this to be over. She just wanted a chance to live again.

Pulling her knees up to her chest, Ashley began to sob. Aaron's arms wrapped around her like an envelope.

"How are you?" Charlotte asked, sitting at Jonathan's bedside.

"Good. The lunch was gross, but I ate it anyway."

"Sorry."

He shrugged. Charlotte leaned over to hug him. She didn't care what it took. She was going to stay as close to her boys as she possibly could. They would always come first.

"Aw, Mom."

"Don't you 'Aw, Mom' me, young man," she said, her heart swelling. "I may go on hugging you until you're an old man."

The words were spoken in faith. Jonathan was going to be fine. She believed it with her whole heart.

"What do you say we call your brother?"

"Cool."

"Cool," she echoed, planting a kiss on his cheek.

"Aaron, I would like to properly introduce you to the president of the United States." Flannigan spoke with a smile.

"Mr. Landers," the president responded, sticking out her hand. "It's a pleasure to meet you. Properly, I mean."

Aaron was completely swept away. Here he stood, a wanted criminal, casually shaking hands with the president of the United States, secret service men stationed at every turn. Ashley, eyes still swollen, stood at his side.

"Aaron is a doctor," Flannigan said, "specializing in. . ."

". . .in saving lives," Ashley interjected, smiling.

"As all doctors should be," the president agreed, gripping his hand tightly. "It would appear that your work is a little on the. . . the dangerous side."

"At times. But worth the risk."

"Tell me." She looked as if she really wanted to know.

Aaron began the arduous task of relaying his story—the whole story—to this woman. . .the woman who could make or break him with a word. She listened intently.

"You see," he began, "I've always felt that each of us should just—"

"Do something!" Echoes of the past.

But the past was in the past.

"Do something," he said, looking the president in the eye.

On the other side of the hospital, in the quiet stillness of the Crossings file closet, Blaine Bishop pulled out a needle and small bottle of clear liquid.

"Murderer!"

The voices rang out, echoing through the tiny room.

"Murderer!"

They called out from beyond the grave.

"Murderer!"

With one push, he silenced them forever.

THIRTY-THREE

Don't cry, Baby. Don't cry!" Coral held her son close, her fingertips running softly over the tiny wisps of hair on his head. "Mama's here. She's gonna take good care of you!"

The baby cooed in her arms, obviously content. Coral leaned back against the rocking chair, glancing up from her son just long enough to look into her husband's eyes. They were misty.

He lifted the camera, snapping another picture. It was just one among countless pictures he had taken over the last few weeks.

"Oh, that's going to be a good one," he said. "I think he was smiling."

"He's too little to smile," Coral argued. "Babies this age don't. . ."

She opted not to finish the statement. Let Jacob think he was smiling. What could it hurt? After all, maybe it was a smile. They all had a lot to smile about these days. She wrinkled her nose at Jacob.

"Take a picture of this," she said, making a face.

He did.

For a moment there was silence between them as they stared in unison at their son. When Jacob did speak, it was with awe and wonder. . . .

"We did it," he said, smiling down at her. "We really did it."

"No," Coral said. "No. God did it."

"Where do we stand?" Aaron asked curiously.

It was a legitimate question. Flannigan smiled, giving him the answer he had waited for.

"We just got a permanent injunction for the Summerlin baby. Judge Owens made her decision this morning. Here's her statement, if you'd like to read it."

"Would I ever."

He picked up the piece of paper, reading as fast as his eyes would move across the page.

"It is the job of the courts to address with great care any constitutional issues arising from laws passed. It is the opinion of this court that the Duty to Die law stands in direct violation of the Fourteenth Amendment to the Constitution. No state shall 'deny to any person within its jurisdiction the equal protection of the laws.' The Duty to Die law is, in the opinion of this court, vague and excessively broad. In the case of *Summerlin v. Mercy Hospital,* this court has no choice but to find in favor of the family."

Aaron laid the paper down, shaking his head.

"Wow. So. . .what happens next?"

"The hospital might try to fight it. They could take it all the way to the Supreme Court, so we may be talking an extensive battle. But they've got their hands pretty full. I can't tell you how many injunctions have been filed on behalf of incoming patients there. And I'm sure you heard about. . ."

"Yeah." Aaron had heard all right. Blaine Bishop had taken his own life. Apparently the news had sent quite a shock wave through those on staff at Mercy.

"I've been in contact with Mason Wallis," Aaron said. "In fact, I received an E-mail from him just this morning."

"What's up?"

"Cameron Walker is sick."

"I'm sorry to hear that. I guess it was just a matter of time."

"Everything is just a matter of time," Aaron said, nodding.

"Speaking of which," Flannigan interrupted. "We've started drafting the bill to appeal Duty to Die."

"Really? . . . What do you think will happen?"

"No way of knowing. I hate to even predict. But this 'Do Something' campaign of yours is really picking up. Everywhere I turn I see billboards, bumper stickers, T-shirts. . ."

Aaron shrugged. "It was just an idea."

"A good one," Flannigan answered. "And I guess you saw the demonstration on television."

"Who didn't?" A huge contingent of disabled Americans had recently convened on the steps of the Supreme Court to hold a rally in defense of life. What had started out as a small event had catapulted into a media frenzy. Over two hundred thousand disabled persons had shown up to plead their case. Congress had been forced to respond with statements of varying kinds, scrambling to save their own necks.

"Progress, Friend," Flannigan said, smiling.

A moment of silence passed. Aaron, lost in thought at all that had happened of late, didn't even notice the congressman's gaze until some time later. When he did, it took him by surprise.

"What?"

"Just wondering," Flannigan said innocently. "Whatever happened to that Cooper girl—what was her name?"

"Ashley. You know that. . . ."

"Yeah. Whatever happened to Ashley?"

"What do you mean?" Aaron's heart raced.

"She's healthy. She's free. Are you still. . . I mean, are you seeing her?"

"Me?" Aaron asked, looking innocent.

"Yeah, you."

"Maybe."

"Well now, Sister. . .what do you think of that?" Hannah laid the newspaper down, turning to look at Molly, a smile framing her question. "What do you think of that?"

"What?" Molly asked, almost too innocently.

"The article," Hannah answered. "The one I just read you—

about the court decision. . ."

Molly just shrugged. "I knew it all along."

"Knew what?"

"Knew all of this talk about dying would blow over."

"Oh, you did?" Hannah questioned. "Really now, Molly. . ."

"I tried to tell you not to worry," Molly interrupted smugly. "Everything always works out for the best."

"You tried to tell me that, did you?" Hannah asked coolly.

"Sure," Molly said, picking up the paper. "You worry too much. Always have. You need to be more like me. . . . Have a little faith!"

Hannah grinned, in spite of herself.

"I feel like a walk," Molly said, standing. "Will you join me?"

"Only if I can wear my purple hat," Hannah answered, looking her older sister in the eye.

"Not this time," Molly answered, shaking her head.

"Why, Molly Gilbert," Hannah barely got the words out before Molly plopped the infamous purple hat onto her own head.

"If you don't mind," Molly said.

"Mind? . . ." Hannah asked.

Of course she didn't mind.

"God is good," Mason said, slipping his arm around Abbey's waist. "But, then again, I think most of us already knew that."

A hearty round of "amens" went up from around the crowded living room. It was true. Most of them were now convinced of the fact. A few things had changed since their release, that was sure. Old Mitsy Jansen had succumbed to Alzheimer's while in custody. June Ann had moved back home, ready to spend her last days with family and friends.

There were other changes, the kind that couldn't be traced with eyes or fingers. The fear factor was gone at Havensbrook, replaced with hope. And with hope came the added blessing of deeper relationships among them all. In a sense, they had all become one.

All but one, that is.

Mason's eyes shifted to the corner where Cameron sat quietly, looking out of the window. Was there no reaching this young man?

If You're there, God, Cameron spoke the words through silent lips. *Then let me know. Make Yourself real to me.*

He didn't have time to finish the prayer. Mason's strong embrace held the answer that he had been seeking.

Ashley heard the knock at the door. "I'll get it, Mom."

She answered it cautiously. The last few weeks had been filled with more media attention than any person could ever expect to deal with.

"Aaron!"

He stood quietly, one arm suspiciously tucked behind his back.

"What are you doing?" she asked.

"She's the yellow rose of Texas. . . ," he sang, somewhat off-key, pulling out a dozen yellow roses.

Ashley reached out, not even looking at the flowers. All she could see were Aaron's eyes. They were full of joy—the same joy that overwhelmed her now.

"Do you know what, Ashley Cooper?" he asked, taking her in his arms.

"What?" Their eyes met again.

He never had time to answer. Her lips got in the way.

"What's next?" Charlotte Tinsdale asked the doctors cautiously. "Where do we go from here?"

Weeks had passed, and there had been no sign of a donor heart for Jonathan. Every day he grew weaker.

"It's just a waiting game, Madame President," Dr. Morgan Keenan said, eyes obviously avoiding hers. "But I think you should begin to prepare yourself for the worst. . . ."

The worst.

After all they had been through, would her own son be

sacrificed while so many others were going free? It wasn't supposed to be like this.

"Mom," Jonathan said weakly from across the room.

Was he awake? Had he really heard? . . . Charlotte swallowed the lump in her throat before answering. He couldn't know how desperately afraid she was.

"Yes, Son?" She couldn't look at him, not with tears streaming down her face.

"Mom," Jonathan said gently. "It's okay. Whatever happens . . .it's okay."

"When peace, like a river, attendeth my way, when sorrows like sea billows roll; Whatever my lot, Thou has taught me to say, It is well, it is well with my soul." The words of Madge's hymn hit her suddenly, almost causing her to lose her breath. They were suddenly her solace.

"Whatever my lot, Thou hast taught me to say. . . It is well with my soul." The words, though whispered, shattered the darkness.

THIRTY-FOUR

Drip, drip, drip. . .

Ashley gazed at the IV bag to her right. Her eyes were hypnotically fixed to it, as if in an unyielding trance.

Drip, drip, drip. . .

On and on it flowed, the methodical sound oddly soothing. Ashley's fingertips began to tap in sync on the rail of the hospital bed, her eyes never losing their focus on the opaque bag.

"Focus, Ashley. Focus," a strong male voice instructed.

She was focusing, all right. What else could she do? A somewhat monotone news reporter spoke from the television, distracting her momentarily—but only momentarily.

The president of the United States was about to address the nation. Any moment now. . . "My fellow Americans. . ." Yes, there she was. "We have been through a time of overwhelming pain in this country. As your leader, I can say in good conscience that I understand your pain."

"Help me!" Ashley cried out.

"We're trying to help you!" the voice spoke again. "But you have to help us."

What could she do? What could anyone do?

The president continued to speak from beyond the obstacle of the television screen. "The loss of my son just two months ago was devastating. But his courage in the last few weeks of his life was contagious. I can't imagine anyone not having the opportunity to walk their loved ones through that process. I wouldn't trade those days, those precious hours, for any amount of money."

"It's just a matter of time now." Ashley heard the young doctor's words, but her thoughts were jumbled. Where was she, again? Why was she here?

Biting her lip, Ashley turned to look out the window. A glimmer of sunlight peeked through the dusty venetian blinds, dancing its way across the room. It brought out the red in Ashley's hair, causing a curious glow to pass over her. The gentle radiance was warm, inviting. Ashley watched, transfixed, as the colors drifted from red to orange, then yellow. Yellow. A vase of yellow roses sat perched atop a small table—an offering from her mother.

"No!" The pain was excruciating. She wanted it to stop. She just wanted this to be over, over. . .

"It's not over," the president's voice continued, "though we have done what we could to press beyond this current situation. As a country, we have overcome, at least for the present, an obstacle of great proportions. I have done what I could in my term as president to protect the lives of the innocent. But we cannot let our guard down. We must stay alert, aware. . ."

Drip, drip, drip. . .

"Work with me!" the president said with great conviction.

"Help us, Ashley!" the voice cried out.

I'm trying! She tried to speak, but the words wouldn't come. The pain was overwhelming. But it was almost over now, almost over. The inevitable was upon her. She was lost in a fog, a haze, drifting. . .

Then words of a young doctor rang out, shattering the darkness: "It's a girl."

Aaron Landers was completely unprepared for the adrenaline rush that gripped him as he reached over to take his infant daughter from the nurse's arms. She was perfect. Completely perfect.

He leaned down, kissing his wife on the forehead. Ashley smiled up at him, arms extended. He placed the child in her arms.

THE AUTHOR

Janice Thompson writes books, musicals, articles, and screenplays—all to inspire others to a deeper walk with Christ. Janice enjoys working with teens and devotes two weeks each summer to write and direct for Houston's annual "Fine Arts Camp" for Christian teens. She and her husband, Mike, have four daughters, each one an aspiring writer. The Thompsons live in Spring, Texas.